∞ THE CHRONICLES OF ∞
SHERLOCK HOLMES

∞ THE CHRONICLES OF ∞
SHERLOCK HOLMES

PAUL D. GILBERT

ROBERT HALE · LONDON

© Paul D. Gilbert 2008
First published in Great Britain 2008

ISBN 978 0 7090 8687 1

Robert Hale Limited
Clerkenwell House
Clerkenwell Green
London EC1R 0HT

www.halebooks.com

The right of Paul D. Gilbert to be identified as author of this
work has been asserted by him in accordance
with the Copyright, Designs and Patents Act 1988

10   9

Printed in Great Britain by MPG Books Group,
Bodmin and King's Lynn

Dedication

I would like to dedicate this to my late agent, Mr David O'Leary, who recently passed away. He was a true gentleman. Also to my wife Jackie who continues to have unlimited patience.

CONTENTS

FOREWORD

Dear readers, as you are doubtless aware, throughout the narration of his sixty wonderful stories, Sir Arthur Conan Doyle made numerous passing references to past cases that were never to see the light of day as narratives in their own right. This has always seemed a shame to me, as some of the titles and premises offer intriguing opportunities and possibilities, (although others seemed to be humorous indulgences on his part). In compiling this, my second humble offering, I have selected those references that have presented me with the broadest possible canvas, i.e. those containing the least detail, and, therefore, enabling my imagination to run riot.

Holmes would have chastised me for my indulgence, Watson would have chastised himself for not having commended these tales to print. As for myself...? Well, I shall be eternally grateful to Sir Arthur for his inspiration and to you, my readers, for your support and for providing me with the opportunity to present my second collection of stories. I sincerely hope that each one will satisfy the curiosities of all my fellow 'Sherlockians'.

P.D.G

BARON MAUPERTUIS

*'... the colossal schemes of Baron Maupertuis are too recent
in the minds of the public*

*... he had succeeded where the police of three countries
had failed ... he had out-manoeuvred, at every point, the
most accomplished swindler in Europe.'*

(*The Reigate Squires* by A. Conan Doyle)

D uring the course of the weeks subsequent to our
return from Rome, I must confess to becoming as
obsessed with the subject of Moriarty's impending
revenge as had my friend, Sherlock Holmes. However, I
was becoming a little surprised at the off-handed manner
with which Holmes was now rejecting so many potentially
satisfying and intriguing cases. As a result of our
triumphant recovery of the statue known as the 'Dying
Gaul', from the avaricious clutches of the infamous
Professor, Holmes's name was still ringing throughout the
capital cities of Europe. Consequently we had become
deluged with requests for consultations, from some of the
continent's most exalted houses. This rendered Holmes's
rejection of some of these cases the harder to comprehend.

As anyone who has read my record of that case will
recall, it was during the longest section of our journey, the

train from Paris to Turin, that Holmes finally broke his silence. He had then revealed to me how four years of investigation and deduction had resulted in the realization that it had been Moriarty's brother, the Colonel, who had perished at the Reichenbach Falls in his stead. A gradual accumulation of evidence from across the continent, brought him to the conclusion that Moriarty was behind the theft of the statue 'The Dying Gaul' from Rome's Capitoline Museum. It was this realization that had now led to our current obsession.

Our time was now being constantly engaged either in scouring every newspaper, whether domestic or foreign, for news of noteworthy crimes, or ploughing through the endless reams of police reports that Holmes had requested from his continental colleagues and which were now engulfing our letterbox on a daily basis. Keeping our rooms in an orderly fashion had never been an easy task for our much put-upon landlady, Mrs Hudson, but the overlay of papers and files with which she was now frequently confronted reduced her to the point of despair and a stout refusal to re-enter our rooms until it was all cleared away.

Consequently all our meals were brought, by me, from the kitchen and our housekeeping was neglected to the point of dereliction. At last, when we were reduced to a situation whereby I was becoming anxious for our general well-being, I demanded that we should, at the least, dispose of the majority of the redundant newspapers and allow Mrs Hudson an opportunity to restore our rooms to something close to being habitable once again. Mercifully, Holmes made this small concession and Mrs Hudson returned to her former duties with a mixture of relief and disgust.

During the course of the throwing out of these journals I chanced upon a name that was, inexplicably, familiar to me. Unbeknown to Holmes, and against his explicit instructions, I had retained many of the letters and calling cards requesting his help or advice that he had rejected as being irrelevant to his quest for the elusive professor. Discreetly, within my room, I riffled through these in an effort to solve my mystery. In but a few minutes I had found the item in question, a small, elaborate white card announcing Lady Beasant of Belgravia. The words on its reverse, however, were what excited me:

A consultation regarding the Master Swindler would be most appreciated. Please communicate with my secretary at your very earliest convenience.

At the bottom of the note was a postscript:

Maupertuis must be stopped!

I raced into our sitting room in a state of great excitement, only to find a dishevelled Holmes in his armchair, an unlit pipe hanging, dejectedly from his thin lips.

'Holmes!' I exclaimed. 'Do you recall a certain article from the French press, regarding the notorious Baron Maupertuis?'

'I believe so,' Holmes replied, with an exaggerated indifference that barely acknowledged my presence in the room.

Undeterred by this I hurriedly continued: 'Then you will also no doubt recall a report from your friend with the Salzburg police, which makes reference to a shadowy Austrian aristocrat who has incurred much rumour regarding his business dealings, perhaps even of his being connected to a murder?'

'Yes?' Holmes now raised his eyes to me, summoning vague interest. 'I also remember rejecting these as worthless pieces of gossip, an assessment in which you do not seem to have concurred.' Holmes answered, accusingly.

'Well, it may prove to be just as well, for you also asked me to dispose of this.' I tossed the card from Lady Beasant into his lap.

Holmes snapped the card into his hand and, after reading it slowly, turned it over again and again, while lost in his own thoughts. 'This is a piece of very expensive stationery. Not for the first time, Watson, we might be moving in very illustrious circles. However, there is no obvious connection between this Baron and Moriarty.'

'Perhaps not, but surely an interview with Lady Beasant might go some way to confirming this. After all, this is what we have been waiting for. A mysterious master criminal, operating in at least three separate countries!'

'Rumour and gossip, Watson, rumour and gossip.' Holmes replied. 'None the less,' he continued, 'there is much merit in the argument that you have made. There is certainly more likelihood of picking up Moriarty's trail again if we take up Lady Beasant's consultation, than if we sit here sucking pipes. Would you, Watson, reply to this on my behalf and arrange an immediate interview, while I put my toilet to rights. Oh, and ask Mrs Hudson to clear up this appalling mess!'

I went about my errands with an enthusiasm born of the knowledge that Holmes was, once again, upon the trail of adventure – an adventure that might conceivably lead us to Moriarty. However, at this point speculation was futile and the following afternoon found us pulling up outside a magnificent white pillared mansion in the heart of Mayfair, to interview a peeress of the realm.

In truth, the interior of this awe-inspiring pile was somewhat less impressive than its shell. Certainly the décor and furnishings were of the most exquisite taste and quality, yet somehow there was a melancholy air about the place, a sense of slow and gradual decay. Notwithstanding this, one could still not fail to be impressed by the sheer scale and grandeur of a building, which at one time must have played host to dignitaries and ambassadors.

A tall, elderly butler, well into his seventies, answered our summons at the front door, alerted by our pulling on a large bell chain. He showed us through to a, relatively, small anteroom, where he left Holmes strumming his fingers impatiently on a marble mantelpiece and myself sitting pensively and uncomfortably on the edge of a large, ornate Regency chair, while he informed her ladyship of our arrival.

Holmes and I were somewhat surprised at the length of time we were required to wait for our summons, especially in view of the tone of urgency that had been evident at the end of Lady Beasant's note. However, we both refrained from smoking in so confined a space, and Holmes resorted to pacing endlessly along the worn Persian rug, with his hands clenched tightly behind his back.

'Her ladyship will see you now,' the butler announced upon his eventual return, thus saving the rug from still further damage. He proceeded to shuffle slowly ahead of us, down an endless corridor, to the door of the drawing room, upon which he quietly knocked with a white-gloved hand.

The room into which we were then shown was surprisingly small and dimly lit, for that time of day, with the heavy curtains tightly drawn. It was almost as if the room's sole occupant was reluctant to show herself clearly to us. In that she was undoubtedly successful, though her motives for so doing were, as yet, unclear. It was discernible that the lady was quite tall and that despite her great age still held the bearing of one of her class and creed. However, her features and eyes were almost pale shadows, and at no stage of our interview did either betray her thoughts or emotions. She was seated in a high-winged chair and she waved us, casually, to a pair of low, arm less seats positioned several feet away from her. When she spoke it was in a clear, light whisper.

'Oh, gentlemen,' she began, barely suppressing a laugh at our obvious discomfort, 'we shall not be too formal today. I shall require your assistance and advice and, therefore, should be glad if you would concentrate on my predicament, not on your etiquette. Pray smoke if you wish, also. There is nothing you could ignite that would be more obnoxious than my late husband's infernal Indian cigars. If you feel you must address me formally, please use "madam" and not "your ladyship." The latter is too tiresome and would certainly waste much of your valuable time.'

'Thank you, madam,' I acknowledged, while taking my seat. I declined her invitation to smoke and readied my notebook and pencil.

Holmes, on the other hand acknowledged her words by eagerly lighting a cigarette, and declined the offer of the chair by moving it to one side, perching himself instead on the edge of a windowsill to the lady's right.

'Madam,' Holmes began, 'as my friend Doctor Watson here will readily confirm, I shall have no difficulty at all in laying etiquette to one side. The vagaries of social manner-isms have always been and still remain mysteries to which I have no desire to find a solution. As to my advice and assistance, you are very welcome to both.'

'Bravo, sir! It is rare to find a man who can speak so frankly and honestly to a lady of my rank and station,' Lady Beasant declared.

I could sense Holmes's growing agitation and impatience and politely interceded on his behalf.

'Madam, although my friend is too modest to make such claims on his own behalf, I should point out that he counts dukes and royalty amongst the array of clients who have employed his services in the past.'

'Of that I am in little doubt,' Lady Beasant replied. 'I value amongst my closest friends Colonel Sir James Damery, a dear gentleman for whom, I understand, you once performed a most stirling service. Although a man of great honour, indeed he would not divulge one iota of detail concerning that matter, he did inform me that you are a man who will stop at nothing to uphold justice, that you even jeopardized your own life in his cause. I also under-stand that your own discretion is beyond reproach.'

Holmes bowed awkwardly in acknowledgement. 'Sir James's role in that affair, concerning a most illustrious client, should not be underestimated either. Were it not for his intervention I might even now be languishing within the confines of Her Majesty's less salubrious, accommoda-tion! It is true to say, however, that the case had a most satisfactory conclusion and that one of Europe's most dangerous criminals was rendered harmless as a result I might add that you may expect the same level of discretion from both myself and my colleague here, Dr Watson.

'Now, madam, in the most exact and concise terms, please outline the circumstances and events that have led you to seek my assistance and advice upon this matter. Perhaps you might begin by explaining why you have arranged your curtains and lighting in such a way as to render your features as almost invisible to us?'

'That is easy enough to explain, Mr Holmes, although it embarrasses me enough to do so. However, to establish a level of frankness and honesty, between us, I shall tell you in spite of that. Because you have the language and manners of a bohemian, yet possess the cynicism of a detective, I am sure you suspect me of shielding my features because there are aspects of what I am about to tell you that I do not wish you to fully understand. The truth of the matter, however, is that the sudden and heartbreaking demise of my dear husband manifested itself in large, unsightly red eruptions upon my skin, which it pains me to reveal to others. Therefore, even at the risk of arousing your suspicions, we shall continue to suffer this unsatisfactory light. If you do not wish to continue on that basis I shall bid you a good day, sir!' Lady Beasant concluded defiantly.

Holmes waved her remarks aside. 'That will not be necessary, madam. Pray proceed.'

With a rustle of her silk skirt, Lady Beasant adjusted her seating position, and sipped from a glass of water, which she then replaced on to a small rosewood table next to her chair. Her delay indicated that the imparting of the information that she wished us to hear would prove to be painful to her. Nevertheless, she persevered.

'Gentlemen, at the outset, I must inform you that my late husband was a most kind and devoted spouse and that not once during the twenty-six years of our marriage did I have cause to regret even one of them. He was a true and honourable gentleman and conducted himself accordingly in every aspect of our lives … save one. His judgement, when it came to conducting our business affairs, was appalling! I should explain that it was only necessary for us to become involved in any sort of commercial dealings because the estate that we had inherited from my father-in-law, the baronet, was considerably smaller than we had been led to expect.

'We were therefore left with a simple choice. We could either sell up the almost derelict house in which you now find yourselves, and give up the way of life we had both enjoyed for many years, or sell off our neglected farming estate in Yorkshire. As I am sure you now observe, we chose the latter course, with a view to reinvesting the funds that it realized, in a more lucrative commercial venture. One that, we had hoped, would be profitable enough to enable us to maintain our current life style here in London.

'Our solicitor and adviser, approved of our proposal, although an independent appraisal of the estate in Yorkshire did indicate that under efficient management the farm could soon be returned to making a handsome profit. However, neither my husband nor I could envisage ourselves living or enjoying the life of the Northern landed gentry, and we would not be swayed from our decision.'

'The name of your solicitors would be…?' Holmes briefly interrupted, while Lady Beasant took a sip of her water once more.

She delicately touched her lips with a small embroidered handkerchief, before replying.

'The firm is Collins, Brinkblatt and Collins of Cheapside, although our affairs were handled personally by the elder Nicholas Collins himself.'

Holmes indicated that I should make an entry of this in my notebook, which I duly did.

'Thank you, madam,' I said. 'I presume that your husband next conducted a search for a viable alternative for your investment?' I noticed a glance of surprised approval from Holmes at my subtle prompting of her ladyship for, although there is no indication of it, within my narrative of this interview, each and every word and sentence was laboriously slow and deliberate in its forthcoming. Raising her eyebrow suspiciously in my direction, Lady Beasant continued:

'Yes, Dr Watson, he certainly did, although it was not until he engaged in conversation with a certain member of his club that his search bore any fruit.' Lady Beasant paused for a moment while she conducted a barely discernible yet clearly painful struggle with the kind of emotions a lady of her class would have been most loath to expose to anyone, least of all an amateur detective and a common army surgeon. This struggle she clearly lost.

'Oh! I curse the day that poor Edwin ever encountered the evil genius of Baron Maupertuis!' she wailed uncontrollably. The effort had surely rendered her breathless for a moment, and I rushed to her side with a glass of her water. Regaining her composure, however, she waved this disdainfully aside and indicated that she was now well able to continue. 'From the instant that the baron's malevolent claws were embedded in my husband's flesh we were surely lost. Through his various business connections, Maupertuis knew of our disposing of the estate in Yorkshire and at once suggested a method of reinvesting our funds.

'Why Edwin should have trusted such a fellow, heaven only knows. He had only met him a few times at their club and had lost a considerable amount of money to him at billiards, a game at which my husband had never excelled. Yet such a casual and costly acquaintance was soon entrusted with the means for our continued security and quality of life.

'Within weeks papers were drawn up by which Edwin and Maupertuis were to be co-investors in a complex of supposedly profitable textile mills in Cumberland. Nicholas Collins, coincidentally a fellow member of the Diogenes Club, examined these papers at great length—'

'I apologize, Madam,' Holmes interrupted in a state of great excitement, raising himself from the windowsill. 'You did say the Diogenes Club?'

'Really Mr Holmes!' Lady Beasant protested. 'Such brusqueness is most unseemly. But yes, I did say the Diogenes Club. Do you have knowledge of this establishment?'

Holmes half-smiled to himself, for, as many of my readers might recall, his brother Mycroft was one of the club's most exalted and long-standing members. 'Yes, madam, a close acquaintance of mine has been a member for some little time and I am, therefore, aware of its most restrictive and exclusive membership policy. This Baron Maupertuis must be very well-connected.'

'Of course, Mr Holmes, my husband was hardly likely to play billiards with someone who was not!'

Holmes bowed apologetically for even making that interruption, and resumed his position on the windowsill, where he lit another cigarette. By now he clearly felt the need to bring this interview to an end with all speed, and he continued Lady Beasant's story, on her behalf, despite her obvious chagrin.

'By now the conclusion of your tragic tale is most clear to me. Despite your husband's own financial commitment to the Cumberland project, the baron's investment was not to be so readily forthcoming. The mills proved to be run down, even derelict and soon your funds were disappearing into a seemingly bottomless well. No doubt the baron subsequently proved to be one of the original owners of the mills and has since disappeared to an unknown location, suitably enriched by the best part of your inheritance. I am equally certain that Nicholas Collins, the elder, is now able to enjoy a most handsome yet premature retirement. If there is any aspect of this affair that has escaped me no doubt you will now enlighten me.' Holmes concluded hurriedly.

Clearly annoyed and somewhat, bemused by this outpouring of Holmes, Lady Beasant collected her composure before replying. 'Mr Holmes, you are clearly a most ingenious if somewhat impudent fellow. Yet these cold facts, which you have so methodically reeled off do no justice to the very human tragedy that proved to be my husband's last weeks in this life. The threat of financial ruin, together with the ignominious effect this would have on our social standing, was more than his weak heart could bear. His strong sense of honour made my own subsequent fate his priority and he passed away full of guilty remorse. Mr Holmes, I beseech you not to let his passing be in vain. Bring this master swindler to justice for his sake as much as for my own. Even if you cannot bring him to make restitution of my estate and I am forced to leave my home, I will accept my fate gladly knowing that this viper will be prevented from sinking his poisonous fangs into another hapless victim.'

There was something about her ladyship's last few words

that clearly ignited a spark within Holmes's cold scientific heart.

'Madam,' he solemnly announced, 'I will use whatever limited powers and influence I might possess to bring Baron Maupertuis down. Dark rumours have been circulating throughout Europe, though nothing, thus far, has been proved. However the time for reading reports and speculating is now over.' By now Holmes had moved over to Lady Beasant's chair and he leant gently over her. 'Be assured, madam, I shall not rest until the threat of Baron Maupertuis has been removed.' With a slight bow Holmes strode purposefully from the room, leaving me to clumsily bundle up my notebook and pencil and follow in his wake.

During the course of our return journey to Baker Street Holmes was unusually forthcoming with his views upon the case so far.

'Watson, as you are aware, my position in society as a criminologist has given me a unique advantage over, say a banker, in being able to observe the various, inherent flaws and weaknesses in the make-up of human kind. My own profession would barely exist were it not for these and, it is equally dependent on those scurrilous individuals who prey upon these weaknesses. Of all living beings we are almost unique in our desire for riches and the accumulation of property. We are the only creatures in our world, who kill when they are not hungry. We are the only ones who experience greed.

'Had the Beasants not possessed these traits then, I am certain, the temptations held out to them by Baron Maupertuis would have been rendered impotent.' I was shocked by this assertion of Holmes.

'Holmes,' I protested. 'Surely you are not condoning the

actions of Maupertuis on the grounds of the Beasants' own weaknesses?!'

'Calm yourself, Watson.' Holmes smiled. 'In observing mankind's frailties, I am not giving leave to the strong to take advantage over the weak. Lord Beasant's folly should not cause his widow to be made homeless and penniless, nor should it allow this avaricious baron to line his pockets at her expense. You and I will help to put this injustice to rights.'

'Despite the absence of Moriarty's malevolent hand?' I asked tentatively as we pulled up outside 221b.

'Do not presume too much at this early stage, friend Watson,' Holmes rejoined enigmatically as we alighted from our cab.

As we began climbing the stairs we were brought to an abrupt halt by the lyrical tones of our landlady, Mrs Hudson.

'A moment if you please, gentlemen. This message was delivered by an official courier, shortly after your departure.' She handed us a small white envelope, with the crest of the Foreign Office emblazoned upon it. The note within, which Holmes promptly asked me to read out aloud to him, was as brief as it was forthright.

Sherlock, come to the F.O. at once. National security at stake.
Mycroft.

Holmes's face lit up at once. 'Ah, so brother Mycroft appears to have a problem at the office. As you might recall, Watson, a summons from my brother is not to be taken lightly and usually leads to a most stimulating problem. Of course, the conclusion of the affair of the Greek Interpreter was hardly as satisfactory as the recovery of the Bruce

Partington plans, although it did present me with its own unique set of perplexities.'

'I recall both well,' I replied, 'and despite your initial reluctance, both found their way into my chronicles of your work. Your brother's unusual position within the Government must surely indicate that this new matter is grave indeed. Yet what of the matter of Baron Maupertuis? Surely Lady Beasant's predicament also warrants our best attention?'

'Of course, dear fellow,' Holmes answered, resting a placating hand upon my shoulder. 'However, at this juncture, apart from dispatching wires to my friends in the Austrian and French police forces, there is little more to be done.

'These I shall draft immediately whilst the ever co-operative Mrs Hudson summons a cab for us.' As he spoke Holmes bundled the hapless woman out into the street, before tearing up the stairs to draft the wires. Within moments he was down again, thrusting the papers into Mrs Hudson's reluctant hands, before joining me in the waiting cab. Once more we found ourselves roaring along Baker Street towards the centre of our great metropolis.

It might be recalled by my more attentive readers that the position of Mycroft Holmes within the hierarchy of Whitehall, was somewhat unusual in that he was not employed by any specific department. His office acted as an exchange house for interdepartmental information, which Mycroft first digested, then collated and lastly acted upon. Indeed, there were very few ministerial decisions made that were not first sanctioned and approved by Mycroft Holmes.

However, we were soon to discover, upon being shown to his large, austere office, deep within the bowels of Whitehall that the not inconsiderable burden of so weighty a responsibility had at last taken its toll on Holmes's brother. It was with some considerable difficulty that, upon our being announced, Mycroft raised himself from a deep leather fireside chair, and as he shuffled away from the flickering of the fire's flames it became apparent that the years since our last meeting, had not been kind to him.

Mycroft's once genial facial chubbiness was now degenerating into ungainly folds of ageing flesh and bore a decidedly unhealthy grey pallor. His hair had thinned considerably and he had acquired a stoop to his back that reduced his height by two or three inches. It was sad to see that the seven-year age gap between my friend and his brother now seemed considerably wider. Admirably, Holmes betrayed no traces of the dismay he must have felt at seeing his brother's sorry transformation.

'Ah, Sherlock and, of course, Doctor Watson!' was his affable greeting, although there was a hoarseness to his voice that I had, hitherto, been unaware of. 'Good of you both to have attended so promptly.' Then, lowering his voice somewhat, 'I understand you have agreed to look into Lady Beasant's little problem, but between the three of us, I think you will find this matter a little weightier and of far greater priority. Do not look so surprised, Doctor, as my brother will confirm, there is very little that escapes me, especially in so far as the affairs of a former member of the Diogenes Club are concerned.'

'The tone of your note was somewhat urgent,' Holmes mentioned.

'Indeed it was. The simple fact of the matter is that the idiot Lestrade has been put in charge of the investigation and I would prefer it if you could learn all you can from the scene of the crime, before he blunders in.'

'So it is murder then?' Holmes asked casually, almost

with an air of nonchalance. By now an evening mist had begun to fall and Holmes's sharp, hawklike profile was set off in silhouette against the uncovered glass of Mycroft's window.

'Murder it undoubtedly is and I am afraid the tragic victim is my invaluable right-hand man, George Naismith,' Mycroft replied sombrely.

'Right-hand man, you say?' Holmes asked a little anxiously, moving away from the window. 'I do not understand. You have always been a law unto yourself within the Civil Service and the nature of your work has always precluded any assistance.'

'That was the case until recently, but alas, I have not really been myself of late and it was felt by certain Government officials that some help would prove to be of benefit. I must admit that, despite my early misgivings, Naismith had become almost indispensable to me. As you are already aware, I work for no individual department and Naismith's previous experience had helped to lubricate liaison between the various ministries.'

'Where exactly did the murder take place?' Holmes asked.

'In my office, next door, and that is the most singular aspect of the whole confounded business!' Mycroft replied. He moved over to a set of large mahogany doors.

'I am sorry, sir, but I understood this room to be your office,' I mentioned whilst still writing in my notebook.

'Oh no, dear boy,' Mycroft boomed. 'This is merely my waiting room. Do not be too easily impressed by size and grandeur. In my exalted position it is more important to impress people before they actually meet you.' Mycroft finished his remarks with a touch of amused irony. Then he flung open the large doors and showed us into his inner sanctum.

The room we now entered was indeed considerably smaller than the outer one, though no less impressive for that. A magnificent crystal chandelier cascaded down from the central ceiling rose, and an ornate marble fireplace all but filled the left-hand wall. However, the pièce de résistance was undoubtedly the splendid Louis XIV desk that sat impressively in the centre of the room and even that was dwarfed by its companion chair, or rather, throne. The three armless chairs set before it were low enough to create a grand effect for any visitor. The remainder of the room's furnishings comprised book-lined walls and a small plain desk and chair positioned at the far end and clearly belonging to Naismith, Mycroft's assistant.

Therefore, it was all the more surprising to find Naismith's body slumped over the larger of the two desks and not his own.

I raised this point with Mycroft before commencing my initial examination of the body.

'A good point, Doctor, for that is precisely what I meant before, when stating that the body's location was its most singular aspect. The small desk at the end of the room is Naismith's more usual station; however, yesterday evening he was required to work late in order to read through and précis some particularly large and bulky files. For the sake of expediency I allowed him the use of my desk,' Mycroft explained.

'I take it that was the only occasion on which that had occurred?' Holmes asked and then, following Mycroft's nodded affirmation: 'Was there a particular reason for this late-night work?'

'For the past three weeks Naismith and I have been engaged in a series of very delicate international negotiations. At extremely short notice the Prime Minister convened a Cabinet meeting for this afternoon and this required a summary of our most recent work. It was imperative, therefore, that this work was completed before Naismith went home yesterday evening, to allow the clerks time to make copies before the Cabinet met!' Mycroft replied, clearly irritated at the memory of the inconvenience the Prime Minister had caused.

'How many people were aware of the fact that Naismith was working after hours?' Holmes asked.

'Not as many as you might think, Sherlock. The Cabinet knew the work would be ready before their meeting, but the manner of its completion was not their concern. The nature of our work precludes discussing it with other occupants of the building. Therefore, unless Naismith got word to a friend or a relation, during the course of the day, the only people who were aware of his occupation of my desk would have been myself, the doorman and Naismith himself.' Forestalling Holmes's next question, Mycroft quickly added: 'The doorman has held his position for ten years or more, and is trustworthy beyond question. It was only necessary to inform him in order to avoid Naismith being locked in the office and so that he could keep Naismith well-fuelled with sandwiches and black coffee.'

'I am sure, however, that it is not unusual for you to work extended hours from time to time?'

'Quite so, in fact in recent weeks it has proved to be the norm rather than the exception.'

'Would all three doors to the room have remained unlocked during Naismith's labours?' The tone of this last question from Holmes indicated to me, at any rate, that he was already constructing one of his theories.

This was clearly not lost on his brother either, for he replied: 'Ah, I see the direction your mind is moving in even now and, I must say, it is a thought that crossed my mind also. Surely, then, you already know that the only door to my office left unlocked after normal hours is the one immediately behind my desk, because it leads out on to the building's central corridor. It is also certainly true that, from the back at any rate, Naismith does possess a more than passing resemblance to myself.'

'Most suggestive, would you not say, eh, Watson?'

I realized, at this juncture that I was clearly out of my depth here, but I nodded my assent none the less, not wishing to appear so. However, my friend was not the world's premier amateur detective for nothing and he immediately observed my bluff.

'Oh, Watson, is it not now obvious that it was my brother who was the assassin's intended victim?'

'Of course! 'I snapped, stung that he should have seen through me. 'Assuming there was nobody else aware of Naismith's late night vigil, what other reason could there have been for so risky an intrusion? Perhaps it is now best, however, that we ascertain the cause of death, and also the motive behind Mycroft's intended demise, before we have to suffer Lestrade's imminent and unhelpful intervention,' I suggested, before moving over to the body.

'Well said, sir!' Mycroft boomed his approval. 'Although blundering would be a more apt description of his efforts. I must point out that my own brief, amateurish examination of the body has revealed no obvious signs of physical violence.'

'You think him dead of natural causes, then?' I asked.

'That, Doctor, is for you to decide.' Mycroft offered, gesturing me towards the body.

As I rested my bag upon Mycroft's monumental desk, I noticed Holmes return to his reverie at the window, where he stood staring into the dark swirling mists outside, as if the answers he was seeking lay within their mysterious silence.

The answers I now sought were not so easily found for, like that of Mycroft, my own examination of the corpse revealed no obvious sign of violence upon it. The discovery that I eventually made, however, sent a shudder throughout my nervous system. At the top of the spinal cord I detected a small bruising in the shape of a fine tight knot. Then, under the folds of the fleshy neck, I discovered a thin red line, probably made by a fine silk cord.

'Good heavens!' I exclaimed, despite myself. Then, regaining my composure and in answer to the brothers' questioning glances, I calmly announced: 'Gentlemen, they have used a form of garrotting.'

The significance of this type of murder was obviously not lost on my friend, for he knew only too well that one of only two surviving members of Moriarty's former gang had been Parker, a renowned exponent of the Jew's Harp, but more relevantly, the most skilled practitioner of garrotting ever recorded in the annals of crime. Clearly showing admirable restraint, Holmes evidently did not wish his brother to share our knowledge and nodded for me to be equally reticent.

'Confounded Continentals! I knew from the outset that certain governments would attempt to prevent me from completing my work. Only they would employ so despicable a form of murder. You did well to identify it, Doctor,' Mycroft said, with the red hue of rage temporarily colouring his cheeks. His brother, on the other hand, appeared to be vexed by an altogether different matter.

'Your life might yet be in grave danger,' Holmes observed to his brother, while thoughtfully lighting a cigarette.

'How so? We have already deduced that I was the object of the garrotter's murderous intent, and surely he has gone away believing his mission accomplished. My life is probably more secure now than it has been for weeks, although that security has been bought at too high a price for poor Naismith.' Mycroft spoke these last words quietly.

Evidently Holmes was loath to reveal the involvement of Moriarty to his brother, for fear of angering him still further. He certainly made no mention of it when he extended his argument for Mycroft's continued security.

'Nevertheless, I fear my caution is well-founded. Consider this. To risk so perilous an intrusion, our assassin would have made himself most assured of your presence at your desk at such an hour. You yourself have stated that you have been working most extended hours these past few weeks, and evidently you have been under a most rigorous surveillance throughout that time. Unfortunately your daily route is so unchanging: from your home to Whitehall, from Whitehall to your club in Pall Mall and thence to home again, that such a surveillance would have been no hard task even for an amateur. However we are dealing with well-trained and well-led professionals who leave nothing to chance and I am convinced that this building will continue to be watched for several days yet. Therefore, Watson, would you go to Baker Street to collect my make-up box and disguises, from my room, while Mycroft and I attempt to persuade Inspector Lestrade to co-operate with our little subterfuge upon his imminent arrival.'

Then, in answer to the questioning glares from both myself and Mycroft, Holmes added: 'Obviously we have to convince the press and, subsequently, the public at large that Mycroft Holmes has indeed been murdered. This fact being known will bestow two beneficial effects. Firstly, it will undoubtedly ensure the security of your life, Mycroft, and secondly, you will be able swiftly to resume your vital international negotiations, for you will cease to be under your enemy's surveillance. Now you do see that I am right?' Although Holmes made this last as more of a statement than a question.

'Lot of tomfoolery if you ask me!' Mycroft growled, though with an air of resignation in his voice. My own reaction was to close my bag immediately and start upon my mission to Baker Street. Consequently, I almost collided, full on, with Lestrade as he came bustling into the room.

'Leaving so soon, Dr Watson?' he asked of me, evidently surprised at my hasty departure. 'However, with two Holmes brothers in attendance, I am certain of obtaining all the clarification I should require.' The redoubtable representative of Scotland Yard spat out these words with heavy irony and a malicious grin played on his weaselly features.

'No doubt, Inspector. So, if you will excuse me ...' With a brief touch on the brim of my hat I continued my hurried departure. My journey to and from our rooms at Baker Street was as expeditious as it was uneventful, save for a chance encounter with Mrs Hudson, the brevity of which clearly left her somewhat put out. I arrived back at Mycroft's office within the hour, duly laden with Holmes's accoutrements of disguise.

'Hah, Watson!' Before I had even closed the door behind me Holmes had bounded across the room to ensure that nothing had been left behind. 'Excellent. You know, Watson, you have been as reliable as always. Now, whilst I ready my brother for his incognito journey to Baker Street – I decided it would be safest if he returns with us for the time being – I should be grateful if you would try to occupy the ever industrious Lestrade for the next fifteen minutes or so. Oh, Watson, it has indeed been a most splendid treat. Once he received the merest hint of a significant case coming his way he has been darting frenetically around like a blindfolded whirling dervish!'

'Surely, Holmes, you might spare a moment or two to relate to me the outcome of his interview with you both?' I half-heartedly requested.

'There will be time enough for that later.' Holmes replied brusquely. 'For now, however, our priority must be to spirit Mycroft away from the building with all due haste.'

Reluctantly I retired from the room once more, and went off to find the Inspector. He spared me the effort, however, by calling out to me upon his leaving the security office.

'Well, Doctor,' he began, 'I am glad to have run into you. This really is a most puzzling affair, would you not say? I mean, garrotting, well that is a most strange way of committing a murder for a start! As for your friend and his brother, they must be two of the most inscrutable gentlemen I have ever encountered. I am certain that they are withholding important information, although what that might be I really would not care to say. Perhaps you could enlighten me, Doctor?'

'I doubt that I could add very much to what they have already told you. I am as much in the dark as they surely are. However, perhaps we could take a turn outside,' I suggested, gesturing towards the main entrance whilst offering Lestrade a cigarette. This he duly accepted and while we strolled slowly around the building's extensive perimeter, he clumsily attempted to extricate any clue that I might have been able to furnish him with. In this he was wholly unsuccessful. I was certain that Holmes and Mycroft would have been equally reticent in revealing the nature of Naismith's recent work, and I could not be certain as to how much of Moriarty's involvement in it Holmes would have divulged at this time. Therefore, I decided to lament upon my being treated by both Mr Holmes and his brother as a hapless bystander and expressed my concern at the continued threat to Mycroft's life. This much, I was certain, had already been divulged to Lestrade, for without his co-operation the ruse of feigning Mycroft's death would have been all but impossible.

By the time we had returned to Mycroft's office his trans-formation had been completed. Standing there before us was a somewhat enlarged, duplication of George Naismith himself, with Mycroft Holmes nowhere to be seen. Holmes had eased Mycroft's facial ageing with some greasepaint, covered his thinning hair with a subtle grey wig, and affixed a small, neatly clipped beard to his chin. Last of all, and to Mycroft's obvious chagrin, Holmes had thinned down somewhat his brother's esteemed and well cultivated 'mutton-chops'.

'Good gracious, Holmes! I would almost swear to Naismith's having been raised from the dead!' I exclaimed, barely able to contain my excitement.

'The thing is quite remarkable, Mr Holmes,' said Lestrade, more soberly. 'Once again you have displayed a further reason for us at the Yard, to be grateful that you are working on the side of justice. By the way, I have followed your instructions to the letter and to avoid attracting attention to the building, all my officers have now stood down. It is not quite our way of doing things, but past experience has shown to me the benefit in trusting to your instincts. Apprehending Parker would certainly be a feather in my cap,' Lestrade concluded wistfully.

'First things first, Lestrade. Is the carriage awaiting us immediately outside?' Holmes asked anxiously. 'Despite our theatrics I wish to expose my brother to public gaze only for as brief a time as is necessary.'

'Indeed it is, Mr Holmes, but I assure you the success of your masquerade has eliminated any risk to your brother. Any lingering observer, even Parker himself, would assume that we were apprehending Naismith, under suspicion of having murdered his superior.'

Holmes clapped his hands in a self-congratulatory manner. 'Excellent! Lestrade, I expect you can make your own way to Scotland Yard from Baker Street, for I do not wish to interrupt our journey.' Thereupon Mycroft draped Naismith's coat about his shoulders and the four of us made our way to the awaiting brougham outside.

The journey to Baker Street was, mercifully, uneventful and within a short while Mrs Hudson was furnishing us all with a large pot of hot strong tea and kindling a cheery fire.

Once we were all seated Holmes took up his old clay pipe and filled it from the Persian slipper, full of strong tobacco, that he kept on the mantelpiece. I knew at once, from his choice of pipe, that he was troubled by the recent course of events and that some serious analysis was called for. To my surprise he decided to outline for both Mycroft and

Lestrade the thought processes and deductions that had led to his conclusion that Moriarty was, indeed, still alive. [See the Dying Gaul from Book 1; the statue alluded to at the beginning of this story]. Despite the instinctively cynical nature of both of his listeners, his analysis was too sharp and precise for either of them to question a single word or explanation.

'My goodness, Sherlock, that is a most amazing conclusion you have reached, yet I can find no flaw in your reasoning. From what you have explained, Professor Moriarty is undoubtedly the instigator of this fellow Parker's attempt on my life,' Mycroft commented.

'No doubt bent on revenge for your having slain his brother, the colonel, at the Reichenbach Falls,' Lestrade chipped in.

'No doubt, no doubt ... however ...' Holmes took his pipe to his chair, where he sat, legs crossed, drawing long and hard, and deep in thought. We three stared at him in silent expectation, for a moment or two, until I decided to air a thought of my own.

'Holmes, can we now assume that having contented himself with the supposed death of Mycroft, Moriarty will now consider the matter as concluded? Or will he seek for his final vengeance upon you?'

'When you consider the lengthy and meticulous planning that usually precedes the execution of Moriarty's schemes I should presume that the murder of Mycroft was merely another step along the pathway to my ultimate destruction. I should say that my life is in graver danger now than it has ever been,' Holmes replied. 'However, there is still the question of the "master swindler", Baron Maupertuis,' he concluded thoughtfully.

'Honourable though this sentiment surely is, does not defrauding Lady Beasant of her not inconsiderable fortune pale into insignificance when compared to your own life-threatening, predicament?' I ventured.

'As you already know, Watson, my scientific mind has never accepted the recognized phenomenon of coincidence. In my experience every action has a cause and an effect and only the workings of a chaotic mind would ever view occurrences in any other light. When you consider that the malevolent Professor has the least chaotic mind that I have ever encountered, save for my own, I dismiss the notion that our meeting with Lady Beasant came about by mere chance. Baron Maupertuis's entanglement with the Beasants was surely another ploy in Moriarty's overall plan of luring me into his web of destruction.'

'Surely you will not just sit here waiting for Moriarty to set his next trap?' Mycroft asked, some concern sounding in his gruff voice.

'On the contrary, I fully intend to take the initiative, however I need to discover a direct connection between Maupertuis and Moriarty before I can take the necessary steps.' Holmes replied.

'So, you are convinced that Maupertuis is a part of Moriarty's new confederacy of crime?' Lestrade asked with some uncertainty.

'I should be very much surprised if he were not. He seems to have all the credentials to be a more than able substitute for Colonel Moran as Moriarty's right-hand man. My first task, therefore, must be to find out where the Baron is and manipulate him into thwarting his employer. Moriarty's traces will be too well-covered for me to take a more direct route.' Holmes now relit his pipe and we all sank into a thoughtful silence, convinced of the flawless logic of Holmes's last statement.

Then, of a sudden and displaying an enthusiasm and energy we had not thought him capable of, Mycroft leapt up from his chair, brandishing his left fist triumphantly above his head.

'I must go at once to the Diogenes Club!' he announced excitedly. 'Allowing your premise that coincidence does not exist, the fact that Beasant, Maupertuis, Naismith and myself are all long-standing members must, surely, have significance! Perhaps if the good Inspector would accompany me, so as to lend credence to my masquerade as a suspected murderer, I should be able to undertake the journey and my enquiries with a certain degree of safety. My position, as one of the founding members, of the club, should certainly ease the process of obtaining confidential information,' Mycroft concluded emphatically.

To judge by his brother's response, Mycroft's enthusiasm was most infectious. 'That appears to be an excellent plan, brother Mycroft, certainly one that needs to be put in motion with all speed. Assuming Inspector Lestrade's co-operation, of course.'

The expectant gaze of the two imposing brothers was more than enough to dissuade Lestrade from refusal. Equally, I am sure, the thought of adding Moriarty to his glorious bag would have gone some way towards persuading him also!

'By all means, gentlemen, we must start at once,' was his immediate response as he jumped up to grab his coat. While I procured a cab for their journey to Pall Mall, Holmes ensured that the elements of Mycroft's Naismith disguise were suitably in place and within a few minutes they were gone.

The next two hours passed surprisingly quietly. For once I found myself with little need of further enlightenment, all aspects of the case now being clear to me, and Holmes was unusually calm under the circumstances. Normally a prolonged period of inactivity while awaiting important news provoked great anxiety within him, and continuous pacing up and down the room. However, on this occasion, no doubt because he could sense he was so close to running down his Nemesis, he remained in good spirits and even struck up a few cords on his violin.

When Mycroft and Lestrade eventually returned Holmes remained calmly seated and relit his pipe while they removed their coats.

'Sherlock,' Mycroft boomed, 'we have our man! Not only have I discovered that Naismith was also a regular billiards partner of Maupertuis, but I also have his address for when he is in residence within these shores. He spends the remainder of his time ensconced within a small castle near Salzburg.'

'Ah, so there is the final link in our chain. Our noble Baron has been building a connection between Moriarty and myself, using your esteemed club as the centre of his web. Now show me where we can at last meet this "master swindler"!' Holmes got to his feet while Mycroft withdrew a crumpled piece of paper, bearing the crest of the Diogenes Club from his coat pocket, which he then flattened out on our table top.

Holmes asked me to read to him from it, only for Mycroft to interrupt.

'No need, dear boy. Despite my advancing years I still have some capacity for memory. Maupertuis' last known address is a walled villa, known as The Willows, barely half a mile away from the village of Bushey Heath, in Hertfordshire. A strangely quaint name for the home of a deadly criminal, I would say.'

'Although we cannot be certain that he is still in residence,' Lestrade rejoined. 'I have already been in touch with the local constable, who has informed me that he is aware of activity within the villa. As to whether the activity is on the part of the staff, Parker, or Maupertuis himself, we have no way of knowing.'

'You have both done extremely well; however the task of ascertaining the nature of this activity at The Willows will surely be mine and Watson's,' said Holmes. Then, bowing towards me he added: 'With your kind acquiescence, of course.'

'I should be honoured. Shall I require an overnight bag?'

'It may be necessary to spend a day or two in getting the lie of the land, so yes, a bag by all means and, I think, your faithful army revolver will be necessary.' Then, turning once more to his brother and Lestrade, Holmes asked: 'I do not suppose that your research extended to train times to and accommodation in the village?'

'Bradshaw indicates that there will not be another train to Bushey Heath until 11.03 tomorrow morning from King's Cross,' Mycroft replied. 'As for accommodation, well, I think I can leave at least one thing for my younger brother to arrange for himself!'

'Well, there is certainly nothing left for us to accomplish at this hour. I am more than comfortable in my chair, so Mycroft may use my room for the next couple of nights,' Holmes observed. 'Lestrade, please be prepared for an unscheduled journey to Hertfordshire, if called upon during the next forty-eight hours.'

'I shall certainly clear my desk and await word from you. Goodnight, gentlemen.' Lestrade doffed his hat as he took his leave. The sleeping arrangements were as prescribed by Holmes and we awoke early the following morning, allowing us enough time for a light breakfast before taking a cab to King's Cross. Mycroft pledged to remain safely within the confines of our rooms up to our return from Bushey Heath, although it was hard for a man of such fixed routine to undergo so dramatic a change to his schedule.

Our train departed at exactly the time predicted by both Mycroft and Bradshaw and by lunchtime we were enjoying a most charming stroll from the station through a leafy lane towards the tiny village that was our destination. The only tavern in the village, the Queen's Arms, afforded us a couple of comfortable rooms and, as we were to discover later that day, some fine, wholesome, rural cuisine.

'As I have explained to you in the past, I can glean more information from ordinary folk in the familiar surroundings of their favourite inn, than any amount of more formal investigations might ever produce. However, the saloon will be almost empty at this time of day, so I suggest that a brief reconnoitre of The Willows might be in order while we still have some decent light,' Holmes recommended shortly after we had unpacked and changed.

'By all means,' I agreed, though secretly hankering for some lunch before our departure. Perhaps sensing this, Holmes persuaded our landlord to supply us with a large slab of cheese and some bread before we left and he was certainly amused by the avidity with which I consumed it. We stopped off at the tiny post office to make arrangements for any messages or wires that they might receive addressed to us, to be delivered immediately for our atten-

tion at the Queen's Arms. From there we took directions to
The Willows.

Lestrade's information proved to be accurate, for our
walk along the narrow, muddy dirt track was certainly less
than half a mile, although the fact that it was, evidently,
seldom used made us glad of our heavy walking boots.
Within a short while a high, ivy-clad wall came into view;
indeed, its height precluded any view of the low-built villa
beyond it from the track outside. The track was brought to
an abrupt end by a pair of formidable iron gates, which
were topped by a set of spikes.

'Judging by the state of this track and the less than
welcoming entrance to his estate, I would say that the good
Baron is not one who greets his visitors warmly.' I
commented.

'Oh, Watson!' Holmes hissed impatiently. 'You see all that
I see, but simply do not observe. We have arrived with
barely enough time to avert Maupertuis's imminent departure. If we had been but a little later we should have lost
our only trail to the most dangerous criminal in Europe!'

I shook my bewildered head. 'I am sorry, I do not understand how you have reached this conclusion.'

'Tut, see here …' Holmes now crouched down on his
haunches. 'There are surely three distinct lines of wheel
tracks etched into the mud, here, here and here.' As Holmes
pointed to them I could just make out their outline, but could
not distinguish one set from another; however I continued
to watch and listen attentively. 'As you can see, from the
direction in which the mud piles have been pushed up, two
sets are moving in the direction of the gates and one is
moving away. From the distance between each wheel I can
gauge that one vehicle is a cart whilst the other is undoubt-

edly a medium-sized trap, each pulled by a well-shod horse. However, the most significant piece of information, that I can deduce from these tracks, comes from their depth. The only vehicle to have made a return journey, so far, is the cart which was clearly unladen prior to its arrival. See here, though, how much deeper the tracks are sunk upon the cart's departure!'

'Of course!' I exclaimed upon sudden realization. 'Maupertuis is preparing to vacate the villa!'

'Exactly, although the precise timing of his departure is, as yet, unclear to me. The trap has undoubtedly been arranged for himself, perhaps one other, and a few pieces of personal luggage. Considering the hour, I think it most unlikely that his departure is scheduled for before the morning, although this we should be able to confirm upon making enquiries at the village livery. As we are here, however ...' Holmes suddenly strode towards a section of the wall that was partly obscured by an overhanging willow tree. He removed his hacking jacket, which he threw towards me to hold, and began climbing up the ivy that was well rooted into the wall. He lost his footing once or twice, but otherwise made good progress.

'Have a care Holmes!' I called anxiously, whilst casting my gaze about lest we were being observed by unfriendly eyes. Upon reaching the top of the wall. Holmes rested his elbows while he observed the villa for a moment or two. Then he simply dropped straight down, landing softly and silently in the undergrowth at my feet.

Appearing well pleased with himself, Holmes cheerfully brushed himself down before reclaiming his jacket from my grasp.

'A brisk walk in the Hertfordshire countryside and a

short, though illuminating, climb has certainly done wonders for my appetite. There is now no need for me to question our fellow guests this evening, so I suggest we simply enjoy their company and some pie and ale. Though, beforehand, we must send an urgent wire to Lestrade to ensure that he is on the first available train on the morrow.' With that Holmes turned on his heel and began walking briskly back towards the village.

I made up sufficient ground to engage him in conversation. 'Evidently you saw something from your vantage point at the top of the wall that has altered your view of the situation. Would you not care to share it with me?'

Holmes let up, from his breakneck progress, to turn towards me. 'Watson, I have not just seen something, I have seen everything! I have not only confirmed the presence of the trap that I deduced from the tracks in the mud, but I was witness to its being loaded by none other than my old friend Parker the garrotter.'

'Good heavens, Holmes!' I cried. 'Should we not go back and make an immediate arrest? After all, the man is surely a proven murderer who might yet make good an escape if we were to await Lestrade's arrival from London. Besides which, if we were to question him now might he not lead us to Maupertuis and hence to Moriarty himself!?' I speculated.

'Calm yourself, Watson,' Holmes quietly reassured me. 'Parker was not alone. He was being directed in his efforts at loading the trap, by a tall figure almost lost in the shadows of the front doorway. I could just make out a large Germanic moustache and a luxurious house-robe, which indicates to me that the man has no intention of vacating the property until the morning. Besides, the contents of the cart have, in all probability, been deposited at the railway station and there will be no further train until the morning. I am sure that this man is the Baron Maupertuis, of ill-repute.'

By now we had resumed a more sedate progress towards the village. Before long, as we rounded a bend in the track, the villa was once more lost to our vision.

'Do you not find it most odd to discover these two so diverse rogues, embosomed together in the middle of the Hertfordshire countryside?' I asked.

'On the contrary, I find it most natural when you consider that they have both been employed by Moriarty in bringing down his vengeance upon me. Maupertuis first lured me into the web by involving me in the affairs of the Beasants, whilst Parker's supposed murder of my brother was the next stage towards my entrapment. We are here now to set in motion Moriarty's, as yet unknown, end game. But wait!' Holmes suddenly raised a forefinger to urge me to immediate silence. We stopped in our tracks and I strained my ears to detect whatever sound had first alerted Holmes. Sure enough, the slow, soft thuds of a horse's hoofs, making their way towards us on the track, soon became audible to me.

'Evidently, Maupertuis has decided that the remainder of his belongings should also precede him to the station.' Holmes whispered softly to me. 'Quickly, Watson! Get behind those bushes and ensure that your revolver is primed, then take your lead from me.'

Without question or hesitation I threw myself down behind a thick growth of brambles and saw Holmes do like-wise behind a similar thicket on the opposite side of the track. I pulled out my revolver and ensured that each chamber of the barrel was loaded and primed for immediate discharge. Then I turned to face towards the direction of the approaching horse and trap.

Sure enough, within a moment or two, a small, fully laden trap pulled by a single horse came into view from around the bend. Its driver was a surly-looking scoundrel clad in a bright-chequered jacket and a battered bowler hat. The moustache that he sported was both dishevelled and lopsided and his curve-stemmed pipe was unlit. He sat there, oblivious to our presence, nonchalantly flicking the horse's back with the reins from time to time. This, then, was the lethally talented Parker, one of Moriarty's staunchest allies.

We waited for what seemed to be an eternity, until the trap was alongside our respective bushes, before making our move. When we did it was as sudden as it was decisive. With no indication to me, Holmes leapt out from behind his bush and made directly for the slow-moving horse. With no intention of harming the animal, Holmes attempted to strangle the horse by pulling against its throat with the bridle. This had the desired effect of causing the beast to rear up on to its hindlegs, causing the trap partially to up-end. Various pieces of baggage began cascading on to the mud below, followed by the hapless driver, who evidently injured his shoulder in the process. I now strode forward and pressed the muzzle of my revolver against the side of his head and with sufficient force as to leave Parker in no doubt as to the futility of any resistance.

Fortunately in this I was successful and, after some virulent and repeated cursing, Parker was both silent and motionless for the duration of our journey back to Bushey Heath. Holmes led the horse while I sat beside Parker on the trap, ensuring that my revolver remained pressed against his head until we arrived safely at the small local constabulary building. The officer was considerably put out by our intrusion, for it had been many years since his solitary cell had played host to a criminal of any description, far less a much sought-after murderer. However, we eventually calmed his nerves by assuring him that Inspector Lestrade of the Yard would be arriving on the first available morning train to relieve him of his charge.

Not surprisingly, in view of his employer's reputation for being able to smooth the course of justice for those of his minions who fell into the hands of the law, Parker was loath to impart any information to us that we asked of him. Despairing of making any progress, therefore, and after ensuring that Parker was securely incarcerated for the night, we repaired to the Queen's Arms for some alimentary fortification.

This took the shape of a game pie, some parsley potatoes and a tankard of local ale. Throughout the consumption of this most welcome repast, Holmes outlined to me the remainder of his plan.

'As you know, Watson,' he began whilst lighting a cigarette, 'at the outset I fully intended to await Lestrade's arrival before forcing the issue with Maupertuis, merely using our first hours here to discover how things truly stood. I am sure you will realize that this is not now possible. I have no way of knowing whether Parker was intending to return to The Willows after off-loading the baggage this evening, or to go back for Maupertuis tomorrow morning. Were I to await Lestrade and it turned out that Parker was expected back this evening, his continued absence would alert Maupertuis to there being something amiss, perhaps provoking him to elude us by slinking away during the night. Clearly I cannot afford to let this happen. 'Therefore, I propose that you await Lestrade here in the village, so being able to lead him to The Willows immediately upon his arrival. In the meantime I shall make my way back to the villa at once to ensure that Maupertuis does not depart prematurely. Before you raise your most understandable objections, let me assure you here and now that I shall take no action until you both join me, unless it becomes absolutely necessary.'

I nodded my head gravely. 'Although I am not pleased at these arrangements, I understand why they are necessary. However, be assured that if I receive word of any delay on Lestrade's part I shall feel at liberty to join you on my own.'

'Agreed, and I shall be more than pleased to have your company!' With that Holmes dramatically stubbed out his cigarette into the remains of his pie and strode purposefully from the room.

The remainder of the evening and the subsequent night passed slowly for me, as might be imagined. Clearly the knowledge that Holmes's fate lay very much in the balance precluded any inclination for, or even any possibility of, sleep. Therefore I was resigned to spending these long hours in the somewhat uncomfortable armchair in my bedroom, smoking incessantly on my pipe. The chiming clock, housed in the dining room downstairs, had just sounded fifteen minutes past two of the morning when, to my great surprise, the somewhat bedraggled, but none the less most welcome, apparition of Inspector Lestrade burst suddenly into my room!

'Lestrade!' I exclaimed, leaping from my chair. 'We were not expecting you until the morning train had arrived!'

'I know, Dr Watson,' answered Lestrade breathlessly, 'but such is the bizarre and urgent nature of a wire that I have received from the Salzburg police that I had no choice but to procure the use of a four-horse carriage. Where is Mr Holmes?'

I proceeded to outline briefly the events leading to our arrest of Parker in explanation of the reasons for Holmes's return to The Willows, alone at such an hour.

'Oh, but Dr Watson, we must go to him at once. He is in the gravest danger! My carriage awaits us outside.'

I needed no prompting and it was not until we were tearing along that muddy track that Lestrade produced that portentous wire. It read:

THE CORPSE OF THE MAN KNOWN TO SOME AS BARON MAUPERTUIS HAS BEEN DISCOVERED IN THE CELLAR OF HIS FIRE-RAVAGED CASTLE STOP DEATH OCCURRED FORTY EIGHT HOURS AGO STOP REPORTS OF HIS BEING IN YOUR COUNTRY UNFOUNDED STOP

'Clearly Professor Moriarty has covered his traces with a most ruthless efficiency. Once Maupertuis had ceased to be of any more use, he had him eliminated. Yet you tell me that Mr Holmes clearly saw him at the villa. I do not understand,' Lestrade said, shaking his head.

'Is it not now obvious to you, Lestrade!' I shouted in desperation, 'the other man that Holmes saw was none other than Moriarty disguised as Maupertuis! Obviously he did not intend making his final departure until he had destroyed Holmes, so he fully expected Parker to return tonight to aid him in this.' Whilst I was talking I checked my revolver once more. 'As soon as he realizes that Parker will not be returning he will surely be in little doubt that Holmes is close at hand.'

When we reached the villa the large gates were standing ominously open. A steady rain had begun to fall, obscuring the building in the distance. Then, as we drew closer, we could see a single light faintly illuminating a window on the upper floor. The silhouette of a tall man walking before it was the only indication of activity. We both alighted from the carriage before the driver had even drawn up the horses, burst through the partly opened doors and then ran up the stairs at a sprint. Fearful anticipation of what we might discover spurred me on to almost super-human efforts and I reached the top of the stairs well before Lestrade, my gun poised in my right hand.

I paused on the landing momentarily to ascertain from under which door shone the lonely shard of light. Then, upon Lestrade's arrival, we both moved stealthily towards it. I became aware of a tremor in my gun hand, but I realized that it had not been brought on by fear of confrontation, rather the dread of any harm having befallen my friend.

Then the all-embracing silence was shattered by the sound of a solitary pistol shot that echoed out from behind the very door we were approaching. I froze for an instant, aware now of my pounding heart and a cold sweat trickling down my back. I tried to block out the awful vision of what might await us behind that door. I could not contain myself any longer and rushed to the door, firing at the lock in order to release it. Lestrade crashed his boot against the shattered door which then hung open. For a moment I dared not enter, and allowed Lestrade to go through ahead of me. Then, mercifully, when at the limit of my despair, I heard a familiar voice:

'Ah, Lestrade, your mistiming is as impeccable as ever!'

It was with an indescribable relief that I now hurried expectantly into the room, although, unlike my friend, I could not disguise my emotions.

'Holmes! It is you! I cannot believe that you are standing there, before me, alive and well.' I exclaimed. Realizing how fraught I had been, Holmes walked over to me and placed his hand upon my shoulder.

'Though misplaced, fortunately your concern for my safety and well-being is most touching. Watson, you are a true friend, but as you can see it is Professor Moriarty who is with us no more!'

I moved over to a large desk by the window, whereon lay the professor's remains. He had certainly been a tall man and even in his contorted position I could see the severely rounded shoulders that Holmes had previously described to me. However the rest of his appearance belied these suggestions of ageing. The man before me had a full head of hair, not receded, and sported a large bushy moustache. There was a large bullet hole in his forehead that told of a point-blank shot and the remnants of the greatest criminal brain of his generation were now splattered on to the curtains behind him.

When I voiced my observations and read to Holmes the wire from the Salzburg police, Holmes commented: 'It seems that I was not the only master of disguise. Moriarty was surely my Nemesis in every aspect. There will never be another like him.'

'Holmes, there is almost an air of regret in what you say. Surely you should rejoice in your destruction of so vile a criminal,' I ventured.

'Undoubtedly I would have done had I been responsible

for his demise. However, I was but a blundering fool compared to Moriarty's cunning, methodical planning,' Holmes remarked gloomily.

'Whatever do you mean, Mr Holmes?' Lestrade asked.

'There will be time enough for explanations once we have returned to Baker Street. For now our priorities have to be the removal of the body and the procurement of a decent glass of cognac. Besides, my brother must be released with all speed from what he will see as his imprisonment.'

We spent what was left of the night back at the tavern. In the morning all manner of police officials descended in droves on the tiny village. Once we were satisfied that our part in the proceedings had been concluded, we left Lestrade to tie things up and secure transport for his prisoner and Moriarty's body.

We caught the train back to London.

Upon our return to Baker Street we discovered that Mycroft was still asleep in Holmes's room and that Mrs Hudson was more than glad to see us return. She would not go into detail, but repeatedly referred to Mycroft as 'that insufferable man!' a reference that clearly amused Holmes. Upon his awakening, to our great surprise we discovered that Mycroft was in no great hurry to expedite his departure. Ostensibly he wished to remain until Holmes had fully acquainted him with every aspect of the conclusion of the Moriarty affair. Although it might have been just possible that, for two days at least, he had found some form of domestic company preferable to his repetitive, solitary daily routine.

We spent much of the ensuing day discussing and analysing every aspect of our adventure. It was decided that it would fall to Mycroft to break the news to Lady Beasant that a refund of her husband's lost fortune would not be forthcoming. By the time of Lestrade's arrival we had fully exhausted Mrs Hudson and her supply of tea, and Holmes had now changed into his purple robe and exchanged his clay pipe for his cherrywood. This was a clear indication that he was now ready to disclose the exact manner and circumstances of his final confrontation with Moriarty.

He stood by the window resting his left leg upon its ledge, his elbow on his knee and, held in his hand his pipe, from which he frequently drew smoke. Despite the subject matter, with his left hand tucked into the pocket of his gown he appeared as relaxed and composed as one could possibly imagine.

'Gentlemen, you must understand that from the outset, when I had left Watson waiting rather anxiously at the Queen's Arms, I was convinced that it was Baron Maupertuis whom Parker had left alone at the villa, and that I had no intention of forcing a confrontation unless there were indications of a premature departure.

'Despite the all-pervading darkness, indeed there was not even a moon that night, I experienced no great difficulty in retracing my steps along the muddy track that leads up to The Willows. Furthermore the climb over the wall seemed even easier than it had been earlier that day. I dropped silently into the grounds and crept, as stealthily as I could, towards the house, from which no light was visible. From my earlier reconnoitre I recalled a small potting-shed set back and to the left side of the house. From this vantage point I was certain that I could survey the entire front of the house and thus observe any unexpected movement. I

gained access to this outbuilding without any great difficulty and, upon satisfying myself as to the view that it
afforded, I settled myself down for what I anticipated would
be the rest of the night.

'However, at approximately three o'clock in the morning,
a light suddenly illuminated an upper room at the front of
the house. The significance of this was clear. The man,
whom I still assumed to be Maupertuis, had been alerted by
Parker's failure to return and was thus aware of the potential danger he now faced.

'I immediately abandoned my hiding-place and crept
towards a lower-floor sash window, which I easily prised
open with my small jemmy. The room within which I now
found myself appeared to be a small, over furnished parlour
evidently thrown into a state of chaos by its owner's preparations for an imminent departure. I picked my way
carefully around the many objects strewn about that
impeded my progress and silently opened the door that
gave on to the front hallway.

'The only visible light in the place came from the room
that I had just noticed being illuminated from my vantage
point outside. Though the light barely crept from under the
door to that room, there was sufficient to reveal the staircase that led to it. I managed to gain the upper landing
without alerting the room's occupant and soon found myself
standing breathlessly outside it, contemplating my immediate course of action.

'The sound of rustling papers from within indicated to me
that the person inside was not preparing to confront me.
Then a familiar voice, cursing the name of the incapacitated
Parker, immediately spurred me to action. I tested the
handle to the door, which yielded. I threw back the door so

vigorously that it crashed into the wall, and I strode purposefully into the room. As a precaution I locked the door behind me and then announced: 'Good morning, Professor Moriarty!'

'More surprised by the crash of the door than my announcement, I am sure, Moriarty slowly turned from the papers that he had been packing into an attaché-case, to face me. Almost unrecognizable in the guise of Maupertuis, certain unique physical traits betrayed him to me. No amount of facial hair could disguise the inherent evil of his cold, forbidding eyes. Nor could he still the peculiar, reptilian oscillation of his head, with which he was afflicted. His thin lips twisted into a peculiar smile.

"Ah, Mr Holmes, of course. I was a fool to think that my little deception would fool so astute a mind. However, I observe that you are alone, so perhaps my elaborate attempts at luring you to me were somewhat more successful."

'By now Moriarty and I were barely three feet apart and our eyes burned into each other's, searching for signs of weakness. The excitement and anticipation of being so close to this epitome of evil, whom I had sought out for so long, were almost beyond my control. However I managed to deliver my response in a cold, disaffected manner.

"If you are referring to the clumsy attempt upon the life of my brother Mycroft, I must inform you now that it has also ended in abject failure. Your would-be assassin, Parker, I believe, was only successful in eliminating a hapless clerk!"

'I was gratified to note that, upon hearing this news, his twisted smile soon faded and he turned away towards the window as he answered me.

"Your strange use of the word 'also' indicates that my

theory regarding the loss of the Dying Gaul was sound. I deduced your meddling hand, at the outset, for my reasoning and planning were faultless."

"'Surely subsequent events have revealed that statement to be erroneous. Indeed it was merely bad timing that prevented you from falling into my hands at the villa in Tivoli," I replied without realizing that while his back had been to me he had been extracting a small object from the pocket of his robe.

"'So it is I who am supposed to have fallen into your hands?" Moriarty asked maliciously, turning round to face me once more. This time his right hand revealed his deadly response!

"'It is no use. Your pistol changes nothing, Moriarty! Parker, your last accomplice, is now held in police custody, whilst my friend Dr Watson, together with Inspector Lestrade are, even now, beating a path to this very room. The net is closing upon you for the last time." I stated with feigned bravado.

'Then a change overtook his countenance, as if he knew that he could never face the ignominy of arrest, trial and the gallows. His eyes rolled up to the top of his head and he turned away from me once more.

"'Oh, but Mr Holmes, for once at least you are to be proved incorrect. My pistol does indeed change things ... most emphatically ..." In an instant, before I could even visualize his intentions, Moriarty raised the pistol to his own head and fired a single shot, the deadly, bloody results of which you were witness to when you entered the room but a moment later.'

'Good heavens, Sherlock! You came within a deuce of losing your life!' Mycroft suddenly exclaimed.

'Not for the first time, brother, not for the first time,' Holmes wanly repeated.

'Well, I do not know. I may be dealing with matters of international espionage, but I shall feel far safer within the confines of my office than I ever will in your place. Moreover, if I am to avoid the Prime Minister's wrath I must repair to that institution without delay! Please thank your Scottish woman for her somewhat limited hospitality. I shall send my man for my belongings later on. Good day to you!'

A moment or two later Lestrade followed Mycroft through the door and Holmes and I were left to our own devices.

'Holmes?' I ventured, once we had enjoyed a prolonged moment of reflective silence. 'I could not help but notice that, despite your best efforts at disguising it, there is still something within you that regrets Moriarty's passing.'

Holmes slowly shook his head while relighting his cherrywood.

'No Watson, no one in their right mind could possibly lament the elimination of pure evil, which Moriarty, for all his cleverness, surely was. As a perfectionist in my chosen profession, however, it is indeed hard to see how a challenge as stimulating as battling with Moriarty, will ever arise again.'

'I can understand that,' I responded, 'but did you not say earlier that the weaknesses of man, which you have so astutely observed over the years, ensure that there will always be someone prepared to prey upon them. Surely it is gratifying to know that you will be there to prevent that from happening?'

Holmes turned to me suddenly and smiled. 'As ever you

are quite right, Watson. Yet it is equally gratifying to know that you will be there, fighting by my side.'

THE REMARKABLE DISAPPEARANCE OF JAMES PHILLIMORE

'*Among those unfinished tales is that of Mr James Phillimore who, stepping back into his own house to get his umbrella, was never more seen in this world ...*'

(*The Problem of Thor Bridge* by A. Conan Doyle)

Thned

There was a certain period of time whilst the new century was still in its infancy, when the capital was gripped by an atmosphere of stunned melancholy. Nation, Empire and populace tried to adapt to a world deprived of its revered monarch, now no longer looking down upon and protecting it. We all felt as if we had suffered a parental bereavement and only that long and bloody conflict in Southern Africa diverted us from our sense of loss and confusion.

When I say all were affected, I do so while making one qualified exception, that of my friend and colleague, Sherlock Holmes. Had our new head of state been announced as Attila the Hun, as opposed to King Edward VII, Holmes would have suffered the succession with similar indifference, for as long as he was continually fed on a diet of new and intriguing cases, these were his sole driving force and motivation. Without these he felt as if his intricately engineered mind would surely stagnate and destroy itself.

The fact that the past few months had seen Holmes plagued by the longest dearth of work he had experienced throughout our entire association, made his customary melancholy all the deeper and darker.

Deprived of the solace that his now conquered addiction to cocaine had once provided him with, Holmes's frustrations became all the more obvious and disturbing. He had even added to the bullet holes already adorning our drawing room wall, a use I had never expected my old army revolver to be put to, and was causing both Mrs Hudson and myself great concern.

With a view to alleviating my friend's condition, when not in attendance at my surgery, I tirelessly scanned all the morning and evening newspapers in the hope of catching Holmes's attention with stories of unusual crime and mystery. Holmes's reaction was to snatch each and every journal from my grasp, crush them into a ball and hurl them on to the fire.

'Really Holmes!' I protested on one such occasion. 'Your recent behaviour has become most insufferable. I understand and sympathize with your frustration at not being gainfully employed, but it simply does not excuse your mistreatment of those around you. Indeed, you almost reduced Mrs Hudson to tears the other morning, simply for her insisting you eat your breakfast! Judging by your pale, gaunt features, it was advice with which I heartily concur.'

I was glaring angrily at my friend in anticipation of an aggressive response, but there was none. It was almost as if the fight, even the very life in him, was being slowly drained away. Attired in his purple robe, Holmes was seated in his favourite chair, legs crossed with his feet tucked under him, in a forlorn, meditative pose. His face, unshaven for three days, was impassive, and he merely nodded slowly without raising his eyes to look at me.

I was unable to contemplate my friend in such condition for another instant and decided to take myself for a refreshing walk. Despite my entreaties, Holmes would not be moved so I struck out, briskly, alone.

The climate and the time of year seemed to fit the prevailing mood perfectly. It was as dark and misty an evening as one would expect for late October, and the few remaining leaves were losing their battle to remain attached to the trees with which Baker Street was adorned. Thankfully, for the purposes of my constitutional, it was dry and relatively mild and each step that I took hardened my resolve to help Holmes in any way that I might.

I paused briefly outside Baker Street Metropolitan station, to see if any of the late editions held anything to assist me in my purpose, and there on the headline board were four words that I was certain would rekindle Holmes's interest and might just save him from his despair.

MONTAGUE PHILLIMORE
FOUND
HANGED

Without waiting for my change, I snatched an edition from the startled vendor, and sprinted back to 221b, only narrowly avoiding collisions with the homeward-bound travellers.

To my consternation neither the clattering sound of my racing feet upon the stairs, nor the sight of this dramatic headline succeeded in stirring Holmes from his malaise. Crestfallen, but not defeated, I lit my pipe, sat by the fire and was determined to find something in the report that might have the desired effect.

My regular readers may recall a passing reference to several of our less successful cases during the narrative of *The Problem of Thor Bridge*. By less successful I mean, of course, mysteries for which no obvious solution presented itself at the time and despite all our efforts, and the exercise of all of Holmes's powers, seemed never likely to. However, I have safely retained the notes for all of these cases, and together with those of completed cases, which I do not consider worthy of publication, they now reside within a tin dispatch box of mine, buried within the vaults of Cox & Co's bank. The case of James Phillimore and his bizarre disappearance had been one of our failures.

I resolved there and then to be at the doors of Cox & Co. as they opened the following morning, and to confront Holmes with my old notes, together with any further information with which the morning papers might have provided us.

I was somewhat delayed in the morning by Cox's chaotic storage system and the vast number of notes in my chest that I had to sift through. I was astonished, therefore, to discover that Holmes was still to leave his bed when I arrived at Baker Street at a little after midday! At once I barged my way into his room, and pulled back his curtains. The room was flooded with bright daylight which highlighted the grey pallor of my ailing friend's sunken face.

'Holmes!' I called, 'I insist you rise at once and then join me for lunch. I shall simply not allow you to just fade away.'

Holmes slowly raised himself on his elbows and began rubbing his bloodshot eyes.

'So you are going to save me from myself, once again, eh Watson?' He asked wearily.

'That is certainly my intention,' I replied. 'I was hoping that the opportunity of closing one of your old files would be of sufficient interest to rouse you from your melancholy. This morning's papers and my own resurrected notes certainly seem to make that a possibility.'

'May I see those now, please?' Holmes asked somewhat sheepishly.

'Not until you have taken some lunch,' I insisted with mock indignation.

'I fancy a shave would also not go amiss.' He smiled, the first I had seen on his face in a long time.

He emerged from his room, clean-shaven and suited, just as Mrs Hudson arrived with our lunch tray.

'So, Lazarus has risen at last,' she remarked.

'No less than I deserve, Mrs Hudson, I owe you a thousand apologies for my recent boorish behaviour. Now what lurks enticingly beneath those lids? I am absolutely ravenous!' Holmes rubbed his hands together excitedly.

Holmes devoured his rack of lamb with great gusto; not until the last morsel had been consumed and Mrs Hudson had removed the tray did we settle into our chairs with our cognacs and cigars, to discuss the disappearance of James Phillimore.

I passed the newspapers to Holmes, but he declined these, though in a less dramatic manner than had been his custom of late.

'No, no, Watson, I would much rather reacquaint myself with the case through your old notes than digest any new information the papers might contain.'

Therefore, I began to read from my notes instead.

'There was a particularly stormy October morning when the equinoctial elements seemed to be throwing down the gauntlet against our civilized world of brick, though thankfully in vain, that will long live in my memory. The branches of the leafless trees were being bent backwards and forwards into unnatural contortions and the few brave passers-by were engaged in a constant battle to keep their coat collars up and their umbrellas pointed in the right direction.'

I paused when I observed Holmes showing signs of impatience and agitation. He was crossing, and recrossing his legs whilst drawing on his cigar as if it was a cigarette. Then he held up his hand as a gesture of remonstrance.

'Watson, Watson! I beseech you to edit your narrative,' he exclaimed.

'I do not understand,' I replied. 'I have barely begun to read.'

'Whilst I appreciate your undoubted skill with words, I am not one of your beguiled readers hanging on every one of them. To me your fine prose acts as nothing more than hindrance and obfuscation. They hinder the skilled detective from obtaining the relevant facts that will, eventually, lead us to a solution. Though they present a fine piece of romantic adventure to the untrained reader, to me they obstruct what would otherwise be an exercise in the pure, logical science of criminology.'

Not for the first time during our long association Holmes seemed to take some misplaced pleasure in heaping scorn on to my humble, though rather elegant literary accomplishments.

'I am sure that I have always given due regard to your deductive and scientific achievements throughout each narrative of our adventures, while at the same time making each tale more palatable to the wider public by employing the crafts and skills of a romantic author. I do not consider that your criticism is worthy and I am sure that your reputation has been greatly enhanced as a result of my work,' was my indignant response.

'Of what use is any reputation that I may have acquired if the merits of logical thought and analysis are buried beneath an avalanche of meaningless verbosity? However, I do not mean to detract from your skills with a pen and perhaps some of your less flowery chronicles may have had a beneficial effect on criminal detection on a broader base. Now pray continue, but please employ economy in your narration!' Holmes implored as a conclusion to his lamentable attempt of an apology.

Still feeling somewhat aggrieved, I sipped my cognac and continued reading, though now more hesitantly as I conscientiously edited the less relevant details.

'As you will undoubtedly recall, the most singular case of James Phillimore's disappearance was first brought to our attention by his brother, Montague, whose lamentable demise was reported in yesterday's newspapers. Mrs Hudson was visiting her sister at the time, therefore Billy brought up his card and subsequently presented him to us, just after breakfast on a particularly wet morning.' I should point out that Billy was the butcher's son and a most presentable young lad who took over some of Mrs Hudson's duties during her infrequent absences.

'Montague Phillimore had been well prepared for the inclement weather and it took us several minutes to disentangle him from his sodden outer garments before handing these to Billy so that they might dry off by the parlour fire downstairs. Phillimore had been most grateful for the tea that Billy poured for him and sank down wearily into our visitor's chair by the fire.

'He was clearly in a state of great agitation and perplexity and this was made evident by the way he constantly wrung his hands together. Phillimore was a man in his fifties, of medium height and build and dressed like a solicitor or financier. He could evidently have been successful at either of these professions, had he so chosen, for his clothes were of the finest quality and despite their recent drenching, retained a sharply pressed crease. His prematurely white hair was frizzled and sparse.

'I have transcribed our conversation with him should you wish to hear it.' I suggested.

'By all means, Watson, this is far better than your earlier ramblings!'

'"Gentlemen!" Phillimore suddenly began. "Let me simply cut to the chase. My brother, James, has disappeared under the most bizarre set of circumstance one can think of!"

'Holmes, the expression of excitement on your face, upon hearing Phillimore's pronouncements, was in as marked a contrast to your earlier one of lethargy as can be imagined. You leant towards him as a pointer dog might towards his quarry and, despite our client's obvious discomfort you could not suppress a smile of anticipation and excitement from playing upon your lips.'

'Précis please, Watson, précis,' Holmes urged with an

exaggerated gesture of exasperation. 'The interview itself is far more important than my reaction to it.'

'Very well then, I shall continue with the transcription.

'"Mr Phillimore," you addressed him, "with all due respect, I should point out that I seldom involve my practice in a missing person's investigation. However, if you inform me of the exact events and circumstances that led you to my door, on so inclement a morning, I can assure you that I shall devote my full attention to your concern."

'Phillimore bowed his head in appreciation of your offer and then added: "Mr Holmes, this is not simply a missing person's investigation, for my brother has disappeared in the literal sense of the word. However, I am ahead of myself. Let me first explain something of the nature of my relationship with James. My brother and I inherited a less than successful investment brokerage from our late father. Despite having careers of our own at the bar, we both resolved to turn our father's company around and we established a partnership, the terms of which were agreeable to us both. We are not twins, indeed James is six years younger than myself; however, there is a family resemblance between us that borders on the uncanny. Gentlemen, imagine myself with a somewhat fuller head of hair and you have my brother!

'"Any resemblance between us, it must be pointed out, begins and ends with the physical. That we are both confirmed old bachelors is, perhaps, the only aspect of our characters or lifestyles that we share. Whilst I tend to be quiet and reserved, James is outspoken and effervescent. I have taken a small house in one of the quieter suburbs, so my brother's home is but a few minutes from the centre of town. As I am at my most content in sitting before my fire with a glass of old port and a good book, James's lifestyle embraces the theatre, fashionable restaurants and the attendance at every kind of social event to which he is regularly invited.

"'Inevitably these differences between us led to mutual reservations and misgivings regarding the initiation of our intended partnership. However, I must point out that these very differences in our natures have proved to contribute towards the success of our company. James's social skills have led to the building of a huge portfolio of well-connected and affluent clients willing to entrust their investments to our hands. Whereas my own more grounded and steadfast financial skills ensure that their trust is not misplaced and that our client's accounts are well managed; as a consequence Phillimore and Phillimore is a name that resounds throughout the financial world.

"'Now, gentlemen, to the events of last Tuesday morning ...'" At this juncture, Holmes, you interrupted our client to enquire as to why Phillimore had allowed a week to pass before bringing this case before you.

"'It may seem as if I have allowed the grass to grow under my feet, but I assure you that I informed the police at the moment the mystery revealed itself. However, their enquiries revealed nothing and, to tell you the truth, I do not think that they attached too much credence to my account of the events I shall now outline to you. Inspector Bradstreet seemed to think that the nature of my brother's disappearance would appeal to your own singular taste in crime and implied that the regular force viewed James's fate with an air of indifference, hence my journey to Baker Street this morning.'

"'I am not at all surprised at the ineptitude of the regular force," you replied. "However, Bradstreet normally displays above average diligence and intelligence, so I shall bow to his recommendation and beg you to proceed."

"'The facts, then, are these, gentlemen. Last Tuesday morning, in our capacity as principle directors of Phillimore and Phillimore, my brother and I were required to attend the annual general meeting of our company. Since James is not the most punctual of men, it was decided that it should fall to me to procure a cab and collect my brother in plenty of time, at approximately nine o'clock, a.m. You might recall that the weather was decidedly bad; the early-morning mist combined with a fine drizzle to form a most dreary outlook and upon arriving outside my brother's home a full ten minutes before the appointed time, as is my wont, I viewed the impending wait with some apprehension.

"'Because of the inclement conditions I dispatched the driver to ring for my brother at ten past the hour, only for him to return with a message from James's valet to the effect that he would be ready to join me in but a few minutes. I received the news with a certain resigned indignation, and sat there drumming my fingers, repeatedly glancing at my watch as the minutes ticked away. When he did eventually emerge he stood reflectively under his porch before announcing the last words I would ever hear him utter: 'I must go back in to retrieve my umbrella!' he called through the grey swirling haze, before disappearing back into the house.

"'My mood was darkened by increased frustration and when James failed to reappear after a further five minutes had passed, I decided to dispense with the services of the driver and to seek out my brother for myself. I rang on the bell pull impatiently and repeatedly and after two or three minutes Jarvis, James's valet, finally opened the door to me. He greeted me with a strange questioning glance, as if unaware of my reason for standing there.

"'Yes sir?' he queried.

"'Jarvis, please be so kind as to give my brother this message. Let his umbrella be hanged! He must join me in the cab this instant or we will surely be late for our own meeting!'"

"'Now I should point out that, although Jarvis had not been in my brother's employ for very long, he had proved himself to be a most loyal, efficient and level-headed kind of fellow and a most able manservant. Therefore his reaction to my explosive rhetoric was all the more surprising.

"'I beg your pardon sir,' he replied in his customary quiet, measured tones, 'but Mr James has already retrieved his umbrella and returned outside to join you. Surely he has not mistaken another cab for your own?' There was a slim blue and white Chinese vase, by the front door, wherein James always stowed his umbrella, but which was now empty and Jarvis pointed to this to confirm the validity of his previous statement.

"'What nonsense!" I rejoined. "No other vehicle has passed this way since I pulled up outside, a full half-hour ago. My brother is merely malingering, as is usual, and employing you to stall for him for his own inexplicable reasons. Let me pass, Jarvis, and I shall search the house for myself!" With that I shoved the poor fellow roughly against the wall and barged my way through. I went from room to room, leaving no stone unturned, even pausing to ascertain that each window was still locked from the inside. Then, to my annoyance and great confusion, I had to concede that Jarvis had been speaking the truth. My brother was nowhere to be seen!"

'At this point, Holmes, you caused him to pause and asked him to explain why he had thought it necessary to check the locks on each window, since it displayed surprising presence of mind in the unusual circumstances. His reply was as follows:

"'James is well renowned for his eccentric behaviour and it would have come as no great surprise to find that in order to avoid both me and the annual general meeting, an event he had no great desire to attend, he had left his house by a less than conventional means."

"'Mr Phillimore, you are indeed describing a most singular event and I can assure you now that I shall take up your problem with all dispatch. Please describe your subsequent course of action."

'With understandable and considerable relief, Phillimore bowed in acknowledgement of your pledge before continuing with his remarkable story.

"'After offering Jarvis a thousand apologies, I had to acknowledge that James could only have departed through the front door and that a combination of the poor visibility and my constantly glancing at my timepiece, had caused me to miss his hurried departure. Though why he chose to avoid me and the cab, heaven alone could know.

"'However, upon my rejoining the cab, the driver confirmed everything that I had seen and was also unable to offer a rational explanation of the events we had just witnessed. He offered to drive me around the empty neighbouring streets to see if we could discover James departing on foot. Mr Holmes, we drove around for a full hour, before returning to my brother's house in the vain hope that he had returned. Jarvis was undoubtedly as bemused as were both myself and the driver and so, as a last resort, I handed the matter over to the police. Alas, their response and results they achieved proved to be as negative as I have previously described to you."

'With that, Phillimore completed his narrative and shortly afterwards he reclaimed his partially dried clothes and departed, encouraged by the hope that you would solve the mystery of his absent brother.'

'A hope that proved to be vain and somewhat premature, eh, Watson? As I recall, our visit to Phillimore's home proved as fruitless as that of Bradstreet and his men, and Jarvis and the driver of the cab merely confirmed Montague Phillimore's story. Matters were further complicated by the disappearance of Jarvis only days after that of his master, and my own enquiries at various domestic service agencies did nothing to enhance our knowledge of Jarvis's previous employers or his background. Of course the singular demise of Lord Chalfont, whose left index finger was neatly removed and subsequently dug up in one of his flower-beds, diverted and occupied us for several days during that period, so that the mystery of James Phillimore remained exactly that. Now to the papers and let us hope that they can, belatedly, enlighten us.'

'Your recollection of subsequent events is most accurate,' I said, whilst putting my now redundant notes to one side and gathering up the day's papers. As I began to read from the first of these I glanced up at Holmes's expectant face, his left forefinger laid across his lips, his eyes wide and alert. 'I am well aware of your desire for brevity and I will précis these accounts as well,' I assured him.

This was a task that I was well able to do, for the various articles that I read through contained little new information that was relevant to our case. Holmes growled impatiently

as I skipped over article after article and by the time that I
had reached the *Financial Times* we knew as much as we
could want to about Montague Phillimore's family background and his achievements, but nothing that would
enlighten us as to the whereabouts of his missing brother.

Only speculation as to the reasons for Phillimore's
suicide attracted Holmes's attention and this took the form
of numerous allusions to a financial scandal in the
Phillimores' company. We were on the verge of consigning
the *Financial Times* to the same fate as its fellow journals
when it occurred to us that the answer might yet have lain
on its inner pages.

Sure enough, a small column on page twenty-three made
a passing reference to Montague Phillimore's tragic and
untimely demise, but devoted rather more space to the
story concerning the misappropriation of company funds of
which he had been accused. This had first been brought to
the attention of company shareholders at the annual
general meeting that Montague had been forced to attend
alone.

'Holmes, it says here that Montague took his own life the
night before an extraordinary general meeting, which had
been called for with the express intention of having
Montague driven from the board of his own company!' I told
him excitedly. 'No mystery, then, as to the reason for his
suicide. He surely wished to avoid the ignominy of scandal
and ruination and, in the absence of his brother, could not
face this alone.'

'Is it not most suggestive that his brother conveniently
disappeared on the very morning of the meeting at which
this scandal was first made public?' Holmes asked rhetori-
cally through the dense fog of his old shag.

'Normally I would agree with you,' I replied while continuing to glean further information from the paper, 'but it says here that the company accountant first discovered the missing funds a full two weeks before the date of the annual general meeting and that he was required to keep this information confidential until all the shareholders were called together. Surely that would have been the appropriate time for James Phillimore to have staged his disappearance, would it not?' I speculated.

'Perhaps ...' Holmes stood there in an enrapt silence, thoughtfully rubbing his chin while smoke billowed out from his pipe. He then added enigmatically: 'Perhaps I made enquiries at the wrong type of agencies.'

'You have formulated a different theory then, I take it.'

'Only a germ of one, Watson, only a germ. I will leave you with a puzzle to chew over in my absence. Would it not have made more sense if James Phillimore had attempted to convince his brother of his absence rather than his presence under the circumstances?' Holmes asked whilst donning his coat.

'I do not understand; besides, where shall you go now? Back to Phillimore's house?' I asked in some confusion. Holmes merely smiled mischievously, then he was gone.

So convinced was I of Holmes's ultimate success in bringing the Phillimore affair to a conclusion, that I spent my two hours alone in our rooms in shaping my notes of the case into a form of literary order. However, even in this new form, they shed no further light on the reason for Holmes's sudden departure, nor on his intended destination.

Observing Holmes's dour countenance upon his return, I feared that my optimism had been sadly misplaced. There was no sign of the triumphant smile on his face, nor of the customary jauntiness in his step. Instead he dragged himself wearily into the room and sank dejectedly into his chair.

'I am sorry your enquiries produced so little success,' I offered by way of consolation. 'I presume that the intervening months have further obscured Phillimore's trail and that his disappearance is as much a mystery as it was before.'

Holmes's languid eyes glanced towards me with a puzzled regard. 'Oh no, on the contrary. I met with immeasurably more success than I could have possibly anticipated.'

'Then I do not understand. Surely the closure of so unsolvable a mystery should produce a somewhat lighter mood?' I observed.

'Watson,' Holmes began, leaning back in his chair with a heavy sigh. 'There can be no sadder occurrence than that of brother turning against brother. Far worse, of course, when a single act of selfish greed should cause one to be blamed for the crimes of the other and subsequently lead to his untimely and tragic demise. The fact that through my own deductive inadequacies I should have failed to foresee and prevent this tragedy is, indeed, the unkindest cut!'

'I cannot even begin to speculate as to what you can possibly mean, yet I am certain that you are being far too hard on yourself.'

'Surely my meaning is clear. You see, for once my own eventual conclusions concur with those of Inspector Bradstreet and our colleagues at Scotland Yard, though for different reasons. There was no real need to conduct a thorough search for James Phillimore, at least not at the time of enquiry, because he was never there!'

'He was never there?' I repeated incredulously.

'No, Watson, he never was there, or at least he had not been there for the intervening fortnight between the misappropriation of funds from Phillimore and Phillimore, and the morning of the annual general meeting. Too late I have realized that the singular occurrence that Montague witnessed on the morning of his brother's supposed disappearance was not only improbable but was also impossible. Short of a belief in magic, which I do not have, the only possible conclusion to draw would be that one of the three witnesses, to wit: the driver of the cab; Jarvis the valet, or Montague Phillimore himself, was lying.

'Since the assertions of Jarvis were the only ones that could not be corroborated by either of the others, my suspicions incline towards him.'

'But why? What possible reason could there be for Jarvis to lie in such a fashion?' I asked.

'Do you remember my last words before going out this afternoon?'

'Of course. You said something about James convincing his brother of his absence rather than of his presence and that you had made enquiries at the wrong kind of agencies. Yet those statements make as little sense to me now as they did then.'

'Very likely so, yet consider this. If James had been the guilty party behind the theft of the company funds, surely his departure at that time would have led to suspicion falling squarely on his shoulders alone, thereby making it very difficult for him to escape unhindered. By convincing Montague and, no doubt, others of his continued presence after the theft, he confused the issue and delayed the pointing of an accusing finger in his direction until the time

77

of the annual general meeting. By that time, of course, he was already living in opulent exile, leaving his hapless brother to face the fury of the shareholders.'

'But Montague says he saw his brother leave and then re-enter his home!' I protested.

'That is certainly what he was supposed to have seen. Remember, however, that the air that morning was thick with mist and drizzle and that James Phillimore was partly obscured by his own protective clothing. Even his own brother would assume that the illusion of his presence was, in fact, reality. A skilled actor, which Jarvis surely was, would have had no great difficulty in removing the disguise before Montague could gain entry to the house, and then being able to convince him of the subterfuge. You will no doubt recall from Montague's statement that it took Jarvis two to three minutes to open the front door, this despite the urgency of Montague's tugging at the bell pull. Of course the disappearance of Jarvis, or to use his theatrical name Terence Middleton, a short while afterwards was the final nail in Montague's coffin.'

'Now I understand,' I said, 'and when you referred to the wrong type of agency you meant that you should have enquired at theatrical agencies.'

'My early enquiries caused me to doubt the validity of my theory, but then, at the offices of Casper and Engles, I discovered that this Middleton had been given a private assignment at Phillimore's address, just two weeks before he was to give his most convincing performance. We know, of course, from Montague's own testimony, that Jarvis had only been in the employ of James Phillimore but a short time and, therefore, I now had my case.'

'Your reasoning and deduction are, as ever, impeccable.'

'Though tragically belated, you might have added,' Holmes responded ruefully. 'Although I am certain that so singular an occurrence as James Phillimore's disappearance will one day find its way into your published annals of my cases, I must confess that I shall derive no great pleasure from reading it. However, on reflection, the humbling experience of reading one's own shortcomings might yet have a beneficial effect.'

With that, Holmes rose, and after selecting a cherrywood, his more meditative pipe, he moved towards the window. He then turned his silent and reflective gaze once more towards his beloved Baker Street.

THE AFFAIR OF THE ALUMINIUM CRUTCH

'.... and the singular affair of the aluminium crutch, ...'
(*The Musgrave Ritual* by A. Conan Doyle)

My more enduring and steadfast readers might recall, with some nostalgia, my first encounter with Sherlock Holmes in my narration of the tale entitled 'A Study in Scarlet'. They might also recall that we only came to each other's acquaintance by virtue of our mutual need for decent yet affordable lodgings. The intermediary in bringing these three elements together, was a colleague of mine, from my time at medical school, called Stamford.

I could not, in all honesty, regard him as a close friend, indeed it never even occurred to me to enquire as to his forename, nor him as to mine. However, I still think of him fondly as being the only familiar face that I had encountered during my lonely sojourn in London immediately following my return home from the Afghan campaign.

Throughout the long years that had passed since that first auspicious meeting, Stamford and I had met only sporadically, at our old haunt the Holborn for convivial lunches over which we would reacquaint the other with the progress of our lives. At this time, although I am ashamed to admit as much, I could not even recall the last time that one of these lunches had taken place. Therefore my surprise at receiving an urgent summons out of the blue to meet him at said watering hole, might be well understood. However, my practice had been quiet of late and my enigmatic friend, Sherlock Holmes, had not been seen at his rooms for the best part of a week, so I decided to reply to this summons with my presence. I repeat the use of the word summons because his note was not worded in the tones of an idle invitation to lunch.

There was an air of urgency about it that left me feeling somewhat uneasy, a feeling that had by no means abated by the time that I found myself staring up at the austere portal that was the entrance to the Holborn. Nothing had changed about the place since our last meeting, nor, I am certain, since the place had first opened, close to a hundred years before, save, of course, for the laying on of gas. I arrived a few minutes later than the suggested time and a venerable old footman showed me through to a secluded private booth that Stamford had reserved for us, which was at the rear of the main dining area.

The aged servant left me at the closed door with the assurance that he would return shortly to take our orders for aperitifs. The whole place seemed somewhat darker than I remembered and the single lamp and small fire did little to illuminate our booth.

'Good afternoon, Charles,' was how I cheerily announced my arrival. Prior to leaving my rooms I had dived into my *Lancet* in an effort to discover Stamford's forename and I was keen to surprise him with its use. His chair had been turned away from the door and towards the fire, so therefore, when he failed to respond to this greeting, I reasonably assumed that its warmth had lulled him to sleep. I now repeated my greeting whilst raising my voice. To my consternation there was still no response from Stamford and so I raced around the table and there found his lifeless form slumped in his chair, softly lit by the glow of the flickering flames.

It was in vain that I called his name once more and I stood before him, demanding a display of life. There would be none. I remained still, as if frozen to the spot, in a state of utter incomprehension. Thankfully my years of professional training and experience then overcame my initial shock and I checked his pulse and searched for the cause of death. This was not hard to find, for the crown of his head had received a massive blow from a large blunt object which had cracked the skull, caused internal bleeding and, therefore, instantaneous death.

Before raising the alarm I decided to rationalize this calamitous event in my mind, perhaps employing Holmes's method in my own inadequate fashion.

The blood that rimmed the gaping wound was still moist, so I deduced that the ghastly deed had occurred shortly before my arrival. Evidently all had been well when the footman had settled Stamford into the booth, so therefore I assumed that the murderer must have acted on impulse without having prior knowledge of when we were scheduled to meet. As to whether the murderer had intended to implicate me I could not tell, nor would I be able to until I had questioned the footman. I summoned him at once and noted that he was at least as shocked as I had been at this awful discovery. I asked him how long Stamford had been waiting for me, and when he informed me that it had been for no more than ten minutes I realized just how bold the murderer had been.

I dispatched the aged servant to summon the police and then froze at the thought of how Lestrade or perhaps Bradstreet would view me in a situation so compromised. While I awaited the arrival of the authorities, I speculated that the murderer was undoubtedly a club member as I knew, only too well, how rigidly the Holborn managed their membership. The footman then returned to inform me that the arrival of the police was imminent and I thought it prudent to ensure that no one was allowed to leave the building before they came. My pulse quickened when he also informed me that there were no more than a dozen members taking lunch there that day and that none had departed since Stamford's arrival. The culprit was still in the building!

A few moments later the detective who had been put in charge of the investigation strode into the room, flanked by two constables. My relief upon realizing that the investigation was to be undertaken by neither Lestrade nor Bradstreet was to be short-lived. Inspector Daley spoke with a broad Ulster accent and was evidently recently arrived from a rural constabulary, for his attire had not yet been urbanized.

Inspector Daley was a tall, broad-set man in his early forties whose ruddy pallor told of long days spent out of doors and long evenings spent within the confines of his local saloon. His suit and matching waistcoat were made of a colourful broad check tweed, his shoes were a full tan brogue, seldom seen in town nowadays. His hat, which he had promptly removed upon entering, was a green woollen thing with an absurd feather adorning its rim. Before addressing me he eyed me long and quizzically, his raised eyebrows almost touching his red tousled fringe!

'So, I understand that you are the inventive scribe for the infamous Sherlock Holmes,' Daley began, somewhat sarcastically.

'If you are suggesting that I am the chronicler of the world's foremost amateur detective, then I can confirm that I do, indeed, have that honour!' I responded indignantly. 'If you had researched your facts thoroughly you would have discovered that during the last three months alone, Mr Holmes has successfully closed eighteen of the Yard's open files and that he has received his due recognition on but one occasion. Even then, it was only the involvement of the press that brought Holmes's name to the fore.'

Daley glanced towards his constables who gravely nodded their confirmation. 'Right, so ...' Daley tried to cover his embarrassment by rubbing his face roughly with his broad fingers.

'Right, so what have we here?' Daley's question was redundant, for he was already standing over the body. 'Quite a blow, would you not say, Doctor?'

'As you say, quite a blow, but more significantly delivered to the exact spot where it would do the most damage,' I suggested.

'Ah, so you are implying that the murderer might possess some medical knowledge?' Daley asked, still rubbing his forehead.

'Either that or incredible luck. As you can see the victim has only received a single blow. Quite often in these cases it requires multiple blows to bring about instantaneous death. However, I am certain that you do not require me to tell you this!' I added maliciously, for I had still not forgiven Daley for his slight on Holmes.

'No, no of course not. Now, to business.' Daley cleared his throat and whilst withdrawing his notebook and pencil from his inside pocket.

'What was your exact purpose in meeting the victim here this afternoon?' he asked. Despite his abrasive manner and the somewhat uncertain beginning to our interview, I began to realize that there was more to Daley than met the eye. Upon hearing of my friendship with Stamford and the nature of our proposed meeting, he immediately summoned the footman to confirm the time of my arrival and that of Stamford. He then dispatched him to obtain a list of those members still present within the building.

The footman's evidence had surely convinced Daley of my innocence, and his manner visibly relaxed towards me. It was then, whilst we were awaiting the list that we both noticed the strange-looking crutch sitting unobtrusively in a corner of the room.

In a state of excitement Daley raced over to grab the unusual object and would surely have done so had I not cautioned him.

'Inspector!' I called. 'It might be best to examine it before we obscure any possible clues with our bare hands.'

Daley glared at me quizzically for a moment, but then relented and stood away from the crutch. 'Right you are, Doctor. See here now, there appear to be traces of blood down this side.' As he pointed, I smiled at how deliberately he refrained from touching it.

I bent down to join Daley and observed that there was little in the way of indentation in evidence. I voiced my surprise at this. 'It is most unusual when you consider the

crushing blow that poor Stamford's head has received.'
Daley nodded gravely in agreement, but he appeared to be
as puzzled as I was at this discovery.

Our perplexity was increased further when the list of a
dozen names eventually arrived, for there was not one
name upon it that I could associate with Stamford nor one
that was prefixed with 'Doctor.'

Daley laid the list down thoughtfully upon the dining-
table and lit his gnarled old pipe whilst I lit a cigarette and
we both stared down at the names, hoping for inspiration,
but in vain. Slowly Daley turned his head towards me and
then, somewhat sheepishly he suggested: 'I suppose this is
the kind of problem that might inspire your friend Mr
Sherlock Holmes?'

'Very likely it is; however nobody seems to know his
precise whereabouts.' I then decided to put Daley out of his
misery.

'I suppose,' I continued slowly, 'that should you decide to
dispense with my services for now, I might discover more
about Holmes's whereabouts once I return to our rooms in
Baker Street. I am certain that were he to be presented
with the unusual set of facts now facing us, it would not be
difficult to entice him to come here.'

'Oh, but you are a fine fellow, Dr Watson. It would be
grand if you could,' Daley responded, his mood visibly light-
ening. 'In your absence my men here and I will begin
interviewing the remaining members. Who knows, I may
have something to report upon your return!'

'Who knows?' I repeated quietly as I took my leave,
although reserving my own private doubts.

I was much relieved at finding my friend's coat and hat
once again, adorning their customary hook in the entrance

hallway and I raced up the stairs in eager anticipation. However my excitement upon making this discovery, was soon quenched by the sight of Holmes's exhausted form lying, dishevelled, across our settee! Obviously his recent exertions had left him spent and I was certain that it would be many hours before he might be disturbed.

It was not unusual to find Holmes so incommoded. Whenever he sensed the conclusion of a difficult case, or realized the urgency of tracking down an elusive clue, his energy and willingness to extend himself knew no bounds. On this occasion, however, his indisposition presented me with something of a dilemma, for I did not feel that I could rely on Daley to detain the witnesses long enough for Holmes to be able to examine them, I decided that to await Holmes's return to consciousness would be to waste valuable time. So I instructed Mrs Hudson to direct Holmes to the Holborn with all urgency should he awaken before my return. Then I hailed a cab to the same destination.

Daley's forlorn demeanour led me to deduce, correctly, that his interrogations had borne little or no fruit. Distraught would be an accurate description of his expression once he had realized that I had returned to the Holborn alone. I hurriedly explained the reason for Holmes's absence, although this was of little consolation to the despondent Inspector.

'Oh dear, upon my word this is a puzzle to be sure, Doctor. Nobody here seems to have heard of the late Stamford, much less to have borne a grudge against him.' Daley shook his head slowly.

'Well, they would hardly admit as much under the circumstances, now would they?' I suggested, somewhat impatiently.

'Now, now Watson, I am sure that the good Inspector is doing his best.'

With a sense of relief that I could hardly suppress I turned to find my friend standing in the doorway, looking as fresh and alert as if he had remained on that settee for a further ten hours.

'Well, upon my word!' I exclaimed.

'Watson, if you had wished me to remain undisturbed, you might not have stomped around our rooms like a wild herd of water buffalo. A keenly trained mind, albeit an unconscious one, is always alert to the slightest disturbance of any significance. Mrs Hudson had me on the road here in next to no time!'

'My dear fellow, a thousand apologies! I would not have disturbed you for all the world, although your arrival is well-timed, I must admit.'

'No doubt, no doubt and this must be...?' Holmes glanced briefly in Daley's direction, but he largely ignored the Inspector's attempts to introduce himself and his men once he became aware of Stamford's body in the chair. He stared down at the bloodied wound whilst I repeated my diagnosis. Holmes acknowledged this with a nod of his head and then slid down to the floor with his magnifying glass in his hand.

This was a process that I had witnessed on many such occasions, although I soon became aware that to the unini- tiated inspector the whole procedure might have appeared most bizarre. He shifted his weight from foot to foot and seemed both puzzled by and uncomfortable with what he was seeing.

Oblivious to this, Holmes slowly made his way across the floor towards the crutch, examining the floor meticulously. Occasionally he extracted from the boards an object, invisible to mere mortals, and slipped it carefully into a small buff envelope. He then ran his glass up and down the entire length of the crutch before standing and turning to face us.

'Gentlemen, I must congratulate you,' Holmes announced to my immense surprise. 'Nothing appears to have been disturbed or moved and the evidence is as fresh as when the crime was first committed.'

'Evidence?' Daley queried. 'I was not aware of any, save the body and the strange-looking crutch.'

'Very likely not, however, I have already uncovered three separate pieces of evidence that I will need to put to the test,' Holmes said quietly whilst the hint of a mischievous smile played briefly over his thin, dry lips.

'Ah, the contents of that envelope!' I stated superfluously.

Briefly raising his eyebrows in exasperation, Holmes then asked: 'Would one of you now explain to me the exact circumstances that led to the untimely demise of the unfortunate Dr Stamford?'

Daley read from his notebook and every so often Holmes would glance at me for confirmation of the inspector's accuracy. This I was able to provide.

'Excellent!' Holmes rubbed his hands together excitedly. 'Has either of you formulated theories of your own?' he asked, albeit with a thinly veiled air of resignation in his tone.

'Sadly, no,' Daley responded as he slowly shook his head. 'My interviews with the club members have revealed nothing of significance other than the fact that none of them has any connection with the victim.'

Holmes now turned to me and I thought long and hard before answering:

'Well, whoever committed the crime certainly had a cool

head because very little time had elapsed between the attack and my arrival at the club. Yet the nature of the weapon seems to indicate that the decision to kill Stamford was made on the spur of the moment. And surely a blow of such force would have caused an indentation in a metal as light as aluminium. At least we know from this that the murderer possesses great strength.' I concluded whilst unsuccessfully trying to conceal my confusion.

'Your haphazard ramblings do nothing to clarify the situation,' Holmes observed shaking his head. 'Inspector, perhaps now I might have sight of this list of members that you hold in such reverence.' In answer to Daley's questioning glance Holmes continued: 'I might learn more by comparing the signatures that it contains with the writing style of the note, than you could during all your hours of tireless questioning.'

With an air of resignation Daley passed over the blue leather-bound members' book to Holmes, who now flattened out my note on the table next to it.

After a few moments of detailed comparison Holmes revealed nothing either in his facial expression or by other physical reaction. Nevertheless he now pronounced: 'Inspector, in my opinion you may now safely allow the club members to go about their business. However, I would not recommend the same with regard to the staff, until such time as Watson and I return here this evening. Come, Watson!' Holmes now hustled me from the room, leaving the forlorn Inspector Daley anxiously rubbing his chin.

'I am not certain that our friend can be relied upon to carry out my wishes for any length of time, so I would suggest that speed is of the essence,' Holmes said as he scoured the street for an available cab. Once one was in sight Holmes, his cane aloft, called loudly to it. 'Watson,' he said to me as we climbed in, 'please give the driver the address of Stamford's consulting room.'

'St Bartholomew's Hospital, please, cabby,' I told the man.

Once we were under way Holmes held up his hand in front of my face.

'Now please, Watson, before you start bombarding me with a myriad of questions, allow me to lay these facts before you. If you consider them logically I trust that you will soon find your questions becoming irrelevant.' I closed my mouth immediately and nodded my agreement.

'The points that I would commend for your consideration are the handwriting employed in the note and the nature of that most singular of murder weapons. Have you seen anything of its like before?'

'Whilst wood is still the most common material used in crutch manufacture, aluminium is not uncommon and certainly not unique,' I replied.

'Ah, but did you not notice the unusual spring hinges that divided the thing? Surely they were designed and inserted to help relieve the armpit of the strain of supporting the body weight.'

As a medical man I was loath to admit that I had not thought of these as being worthy of note. 'Carry on.' I suggested.

'I thought as much. Similarly I am certain that you did not notice that the rubber support, at its base, was screwed into place for easy removal and was not a permanent fixture. Your expression tells me that you find this detail of no account, however you were not privy to a minute discovery that I made on the floor of the booth.'

'Ah, the contents of your envelope!' I exclaimed, now

hanging on to every one of Holmes's words. Holmes carefully extracted the envelope from his inside pocket and slowly emptied its contents into the palm of his hand.

'Come now, Holmes! You go too far. What relevance could a single tiny pellet such as this possibly have?'

'None at all,' Holmes calmly replied. 'At least, not in isolation. But when you consider that this pellet is one of hundreds found inside a four-bore shotgun shell, then it acquires a greater significance.' Before continuing Holmes studied my countenance for any signs of my comprehending. Upon observing, quite correctly, that there was none, he continued:

'These shells are quite simple to open and to empty and the combined weight of the contents of only a few shells would be sufficient to render the base of the crutch solid enough to cause great damage.'

I shook my head in astonishment. 'My goodness, Holmes, the things that you know! I understand now. The screw base leaves the crutch equally simple to empty afterwards.' Then after further consideration, I added: 'Of course, the bloodstain was only visible close to the base of the crutch!'

'Watson, Watson, it does take a while for the pennies to drop, but when they do there is a veritable cascade.'

Ignoring Holmes's sarcastic response I reminded him of the other notable point of reference that he had previously mentioned.

'This point will be far easier for you to digest, because there was not one club member whose writing corresponded to that of the note, including that of its supposed author, our old friend Stamford! Therefore, we shall have to look elsewhere if we are to discover the identity of our killer. Now, I think we are close to our destination. A few discreet enquiries at this most reputable of institutions will, I think present our provincial inspector with his first case at the Yard.'

I seemed to be remembered by the officials at the entrance to St Barts and, as a consequence, we were soon traversing those hallowed corridors towards Stamford's chambers. A colleague of Stamford's, obviously ignorant of the events at the Holborn informed us of Stamford's absence, but made no objections to our awaiting his return in his consulting room.

Upon gaining entrance to Stamford's rooms Holmes gestured for me to stand vigil by the heavy oak door while he began an urgent, albeit most thorough, search through the various papers contained in the drawers of Stamford's desk.

I kept my ear close to the door, so that I could alert Holmes to the sound of someone approaching, all the while glancing furtively in Holmes's direction. Every so often he emitted a grunt of frustration and each utterance being followed with an increase in the intensity of his search.

'In heaven's name, Holmes! What can you possibly be looking for?' I whispered hoarsely, out of frustration. When no reply came I glanced back towards him, to find him beaming contentedly while clutching a maroon leather-bound volume in one hand and a rather official-looking document in the other. Before I could ask him what these were Holmes had tucked them inside his coat. Then he nodded to me to open the door.

Having calmed ourselves, we returned to the corridor outside.

'We shall return at a more convenient time!' Holmes called cheerily to the fellow who had directed us to

Stamford's room. We doffed our hats towards the door-keeper then made off in search of a cab.

I had expected Holmes to direct the driver towards the Holborn, so I was somewhat surprised to hear him give Baker Street as our next destination. However, upon reaching our rooms he explained that he wanted to examine the items that he had taken from Stamford's desk, before presenting his findings to Inspector Daley.

He poured out a substantial Cognac for us both and offered me a cigar from the coal scuttle, before spreading the papers out on the table under the illumination of a small oil lamp.

'Let us study these in silence for a moment, before voicing our conclusions.' Holmes suggested. I nodded my agreement and was most careful in placing my cigar in a large glass ashtray, well away from the papers.

The book turned out to be Stamford's diary and the document none other than the patent for the unique spring hinges, employed in ensuring that the aluminium crutch was more comfortable than any other of its type. We had hoped that the diary would reveal some of Stamford's innermost thoughts and thereby furnish us with a clue as to the motive behind his horrendous demise. However, this proved to be a purely professional journal, providing brief notes as to his day-to-day activities. My disappointment at making this discovery was tempered somewhat by Holmes's excitement. He hurriedly removed the note that I had received from Stamford and laid it out next to the page in the diary that had so excited him.

'See here, Watson!' he said, breaking our silence while pointing at the note.

I compared the two and immediately understood the implications of Holmes's discovery.

'Again, there is no similarity between the two. I say!' I suddenly exclaimed. 'Whoever did send the note used his knowledge of my association with Stamford as a means to camouflage his crime. This is intolerable!'

'Calm yourself, Watson, there are graver implications here than your personal indignation. Read some of Stamford's diary entries. Here, on the fourth of last month: *Have agreed to increase Paulsen's share of the proceeds from the crutch to forty per cent. I fear that this may still not be enough to satisfy him.*'

'Now read this entry of but a week later. *Paulsen's manner has become most threatening. I fear that I may soon be compelled to get in touch with my old friend Watson. His colleague Sherlock Holmes may be my only hope.* This entry certainly explains your involvement, eh, Watson?'

'Certainly it does. Yet how did this Paulsen have access to Stamford's diary? How did he know of my friendship with Stamford and our penchant for the Holborn?'

Holmes suddenly got up from the table and lit his cigar, using an ember with the tongs from the fireplace.

'For the answers to your questions I would suggest that you need to look no further than to the foot of the final page of these patent papers and to the very last entry in the diary,' Holmes replied gravely.

I followed Holmes's instructions and then, having done so, laid the documents on to the table again.

'Phew! So this fellow Paulsen was none other than Stamford's partner in the invention of the aluminium crutch. As is often the case, greed has proved to be the motive for the taking of a life.'

'Quite so, old fellow. Too often I fear that the satisfaction I receive from my chosen profession is tempered by the humility born of witnessing the good being extinguished by the evil. Now call for Mrs Hudson. We must send a wire with all speed to Daley at the Holborn. Instruct him to arrest the footman at once and inform him that I will provide him with the details of the case early tomorrow morning. I think that we have delayed the remainder of the staff there for long enough.

'Oh, and be so kind as to suggest that he might search through the footman's belongings, or should I now refer to him as Paulsen? For that is surely his masquerade. I would not be a bit surprised if Daley were to discover that Paulsen possesses a "Gladstone" full of the pellets from some shotgun shells!'

Holmes now abandoned his cigar in favour of his cherry-wood and retreated to the windowsill looking out over the street below. I issued his instructions to Mrs Hudson, who went about the business immediately. During the protracted silence that followed I was able to read again the very last entry that Stamford ever wrote.

I have arranged one final meeting with Paulsen, in the hope that the convivial ambiance of the Holborn might induce harmony rather than violence. Sadly my friend's hopes had been dashed in the most tragic way possible and my thoughts were accompanied by the sad lament of Holmes's violin.

THE ADVENTURE OF THE ABOMINABLE WIFE

'... as well as a full account of Ricoletti of the club foot and his abominable wife.'

(*The Musgrave Ritual* by A. Conan Doyle)

A particularly pleasant spring afternoon in 1890, just a few months prior to Holmes's supposedly calamitous confrontation with Professor Moriarty at the Reichenbach Falls, found my friend sitting on the windowsill overlooking Baker Street, toiling over Bruch's Violin Concerto.

I use the word toiling for that is the only way that I can describe the horrendous, discordant screeching that was being emitted from Holmes's normally sublime instrument. It is worth mentioning here that the last few months had seen his workload of noteworthy cases reach an unprecedentedly high level. The affairs of the 'Enigmatic Talisman' and the 'Venetian Mandolin' are at least two of those that will undoubtedly, one day, be included in my ever-growing compilation.

However, the last few weeks had seen a certain slackening off and, as a consequence, I had noticed certain signs of frustration returning once more to Holmes's behaviour as

97

his nature rebelled against the stagnation of his faculties. His inept rendering of the Bruch was indicative of this. Surprisingly, though, and in an instant Holmes's bow on string became true again and the strands of the concerto became sweet and coherent once more.

I could not perceive a reason for this sudden change until I decided to employ Holmes's own methods. There was a smile of satisfaction on his face and I stole stealthily over to the window. Sure enough I saw our old friend Inspector Lestrade, having just vacated a departing cab, staring up at our rooms standing next to a most singular-looking companion.

'So you perceive a case in the offing?' I asked.

'Certainly the potential, Watson, although, as you know, I am loath to make assumptions without being in possession of the facts.' Holmes smiled whilst carefully replacing the violin into its case. Reluctantly I put down the book that I had been engrossed in, Lord Lynton's veritable tome *The Last Days of Pompeii* and a moment later there came Mrs Hudson's inevitable knock on the door.

Once our guests had entered the room, Holmes sized them up for a moment before reciprocating their greeting.

'Tea for four if you would be so kind, Mrs Hudson. Please take a seat, Mr Clarke!'

The look of astonishment on the stranger's face was certainly mirrored by that on both Lestrade's and my own.

'I was not aware that I had previously made your acquaintance, sir,' said the man identified as Mr Clarke.

'I can assure you that you have not.' Holmes replied.

'Then in heaven's name, what magic have you used to identify me?'

'I can assure you that there is nothing magical in

anything that I do.' Before explaining himself and, I am certain, in order to create the maximum dramatic effect, Holmes turned deliberately away to prepare, slowly, his old clay pipe.

This most singular-looking gentleman presenting himself before us stood at just below average height and his build was certainly more than a little portly. He sported a most lively-coloured waistcoat; a checked tweed jacket fashioned from a cloth of deepest maroon and a bowler hat to match. He appeared to be in his early fifties and when he spoke it was with a deep, rich baritone voice. He used his arms to a most dramatic effect.

As I was making these observations Mrs Hudson returned with a tray of tea. Holmes waved our guests towards the spare chairs.

After we had each had a sip of tea Clarke repeated his question. Holmes hesitated, as if he had forgotten it.

'Mr Clarke, your somewhat exuberant attire, your extravagant affectations together with such a well-trained resonant voice indicates employment in a branch of the performing arts. When I observe a strand or two of straw still clinging to the base of your left heel and a light dusting of sawdust nestling within the folds of your trouser turn-ups I can narrow that down to a circus. Furthermore, I observe a red blister between the thumb and forefinger of your right hand, of the type that I would normally associate with a driver and his use of a whip. You are, therefore, either a trainer of animals or the ringmaster. The quality of your clothes and shoes and the magnitude of your girth seem to indicate the latter. I have observed of late a large number of posters advertising Clarke and Clarke's Circus as being "The Only Show in Town". Therefore you are one of the proprietors of said circus. Which one, of course, I cannot possibly tell,' Holmes concluded with a flourish.

'Well, upon my word! The reputation that goes before you and your powers is by no means exaggerated.' Clarke applauded most enthusiastically. 'I am indeed Carlton Clarke; however, I should point out that the second "Clarke" is merely another affectation of mine. I found the symmetry of my "Three Cs" motif most appealing and so do my public.'

Now it was Holmes's turn to give some applause. 'Really, Lestrade, your companion is most entertaining. I fancy, however, that there is a darker motive for your visit this afternoon?'

'Oh, indeed there is, Mr Holmes,' Lestrade confirmed, 'although on this occasion I think that even your powers may be found to be somewhat inadequate.' For a brief moment a hint of maliciousness flashed across Lestrade's weaselly countenance, as of old.

This was clearly not lost on Holmes, who now responded sternly: 'That surely remains to be seen! However, before we allow ourselves to reach any premature conclusions, perhaps we should allow Mr Clarke to describe the details of his hopeless cause. I assume that that is the adjective used by our disparaging Inspector?'

'Indeed it was, Mr Holmes, although I should point out that it is not for my cause that I have persuaded the Inspector to accompany me here to consult with you. It is for the sake of my old friend, known as Ricoletti, whose nature, I am certain, makes it impossible that he should have committed the heinous crime of which he now stands accused. Namely, the murder of his wife with a throwing knife through the head!'

These words suddenly ignited Holmes's eyes and he almost shuddered in anticipation.

'Watson, I think that this might be the moment for your notebook and pencil,' Holmes pointedly suggested. I could not have agreed with him more and yet I had hesitated, so aghast had I been at the words of Carlton Clarke.

'Before you relate to me the precise details of this remarkable-sounding crime please explain to me the use of the words "known as" when you referred to your friend Ricoletti,' Holmes requested, whilst lighting his pipe once more.

'His circus act is known as "The Remarkable Ricoletti and The Fearless Maria," Maria being his wife. However, their real names were Alfred and Sonia Walker from Bermondsey.'

'Now explain to me in terms as exact and detailed as you are able, the circumstances and events that have led to the dire plight in which your friend finds himself.' Holmes now sank back into his chair and tightly closed his eyes as an aid for the intense concentration that he now required of himself.

'The Walkers first came to my attention during the course of my grand tour of Europe in the early 80s, when my troupe packed out the ancient amphitheatre of Padua. The entire tour had been a triumph and the finale in Padua was its magnificent culmination.

'It was while we were breaking camp on the following morning that the Walkers first presented themselves. This first meeting was not an auspicious beginning to our association. They had, evidently, been unemployed for some time. Their attire was worn and dishevelled and Alfred was badly in need of both a haircut and a shave. His movement was hampered by a club foot. The only aspect of their appearance that was worthy of note was a beautiful pair of bright-red shoes that adorned the feet of Sonia.

'In all honesty, I was so distracted by our preparations to depart that I gave those two little or no attention and his insistence that he was the greatest knife-thrower ever to grace the ring of a circus, fell on deaf ears. It was only when I discovered that they had followed our show all the way to our base in London that I decided that their perseverance, if nothing else, warranted giving them an audition.

'Despite their somewhat tattered appearance in Italy they had, evidently preserved their stage clothes in good repair and when they eventually presented their act they looked impressive indeed. Alfred was attired in a black suit that was richly bordered with a striking red brocade. His club foot was disguised by the great width of the hems of his trousers. Sonia wore a dazzling red leotard decorated with jet beads and silver diamante and the same red shoes that I had seen briefly in Padua, the whole ensemble being crowned by a sparkling tiara.

'Their act was every bit as sensational as their appearance. Upon my word, Mr Holmes, throughout all my years under the "big top" I have yet to witness a finer exponent of the knife-thrower's art than the "Remarkable Ricoletti". His speed and accuracy are unparalleled and his ability to almost shave the skin of his target, while yet leaving it unscathed, borders on the uncanny.

'This much I recognized at once and I lost no time in signing them both up for the next season. It was a decision that I have never regretted. They created a sensation whenever they appeared and, up to two days ago, they have proved to be our biggest draw.' Carlton Clarke now paused as he sipped his tea disconsolately.

Holmes now opened his eyes and leant forward.

'Mr Clarke, you must spare me no detail, no matter how

trivial it might appear to be, as you relate the events of two days ago.' Holmes quietly instructed him.

'Those events are still so indelibly imprinted on my mind that to omit any of them would be impossible,' Clarke reassured him.

'I should preface my statement by making one thing clear from the outset. Despite their teamwork in the ring, the Walker's marriage was not a happy one. There was not one occasion when this affected their performance, indeed their public rejoiced in the fact that the "Ricolettis" were a couple rather than just a performer and his assistant. However, once they were backstage they rarely enjoyed a happy moment together. Sonia would not give Alfred a minute's rest. She was forever scolding him over one thing or another and would pursue him for a new frock or a pair of shoes, to the point of distraction. This despite the fact that her obsession was bringing about their financial ruination.

'On the other hand Alfred was a man of moderation and after a fearsome argument he would eventually give in to Sonia's feverish demands. Nevertheless, it was becoming harder for him to continue with the act and at last, two days ago, things appeared to be coming to a head.

'"Goldie" had made off with another pair of Sonia's shoes and—'

'Who or what is "Goldie"?' Holmes impatiently interrupted.

'My apologies, Mr Holmes. I should have mentioned that "Goldie" was Alfred's closest friend and his only harbour from the storm of his marital turmoil. He was also a Golden Labrador with a peculiar penchant for ladies' shoes.'

'So "Goldie" is a dog.' Holmes stated, clearly becoming exasperated. 'Yet you refer to it in the past tense?'

'When the accident occurred he became most agitated. He ran around their changing room barking hysterically, chewing up everything in his path, until he eventually disappeared through the tent flap, to be seen no more.'

'So you are still referring to the tragedy as an accident,' I observed, full of admiration for Clarke's continuing loyalty to his beleaguered friend.

'Indeed I do, Doctor, but before I can convince anyone of Alfred's innocence I must first explain the reasons for his suspected guilt. Sonia's reaction to Goldie's mauling of her pair of shoes was, perhaps, the most verbally violent that we had yet witnessed. She compounded this by hurling various objects around the room and she insulted Alfred in the most objectionable and personal terms. He was only able to calm the situation by offering to replace the shoes and by promising to give the dog away. Such is the man's dedication to his art that he was willing to make so great a sacrifice for the preservation of his act. Then they continued with their rehearsal.'

'What, exactly, are the circumstances and conditions in which these rehearsals take place?' Holmes asked.

'The intensity of their concentration is such that they always practise alone and in the confines of their room. You may ask why Sonia needs to concentrate at the same level as her husband, but when I tell you that their show, even in rehearsal, is performed throughout with Alfred fully blindfolded, and that Sonia's positioning and stillness is of life preserving importance, you might then well understand.'

Holmes called a pause to this narration by holding up his hand before him. 'You are absolutely convinced of the total efficacy of these blindfolds?' Holmes asked. 'Have no doubt as to the importance of the accuracy of your answer, Mr Clarke.'

'Oh, I have no doubt, Mr Holmes,' Clarke replied emphatically. 'The very first thing that I did before their first audition was to test the thoroughness of his blindfolds. Furthermore, every so often I conduct random inspections, to ensure the continued authenticity of the act. I have yet to be disappointed. Therefore I am convinced that all was as it should be on the night of the tragedy. The camp settled down soon after Sonia's histrionics and the Walkers continued with their rehearsal in absolute silence. So it was only when the dog began his crazed yelping that we were alerted to what had befallen Sonia. We raced to their tent and there found Alfred sobbing inconsolably over the body of his wife, who lay there soaked in the blood of her awful, gaping head wound. Alfred's beautiful knife was still hanging there embedded between Sonia's darkened eyes. The police surgeon confirmed, subsequently, that she had died instantly.

'Mr Holmes I implore you to take up my friend's case, despite its unpromising appearance. Do not let the circumstances cloud your instincts, as they have clouded those of others.' Clarke now glanced briefly in Lestrade's direction. 'Despite all that he had endured in the face of Sonia's vile, avaricious temperament, Alfred was still very much in love with his wife and his pure nature would preclude his carrying out so heinous a crime as he has been accused of.'

Carlton Clarke now sank back into his chair with the relief of one who has been exhausted by his efforts.

'Have no fear, Mr Clarke,' Holmes declared, though glowering towards his old adversary from the Yard. 'As Watson here will attest, your friend's predicament will not be the first, nor, I am certain, the last forlorn cause that we have taken up.'

Waving aside all Clarke's efforts to express his gratitude, Holmes next announced: 'Now, Watson, I would set you to the task of securing the services of two hansom-cabs.'

'Two?' I queried.

'One for my visit to the circus and the other for you to obtain the services of Toby.'

'Ah, I think I understand,' I answered, ignoring the questioning glances of the other two.

I should mention here that Toby is an old canine ally of ours. A bloodhound of unremarkable appearance and yet unerring instincts and abilities who had come to our assistance on more than one occasion, most notably during the successful culmination of 'The Sign of Four' affair.

So it was but a few moments later whilst Holmes and the others were hurrying towards the scene of the crime, that I found myself on the way to Lambeth. Number three, Pinchin Lane, to be precise, and the residence of the smallest and strangest zoo that I have ever heard of. On this occasion I had no great difficulty in finding the place and still less in identifying Toby, for he came bounding towards me without a moment's hesitation. Sherman, the owner of the beast, handed him over, content in the knowledge that Sherlock Holmes was to put Toby to good service once again.

After his affectionate greetings had bestowed a good dowsing upon my face, Toby bounded contentedly alongside me, towards the waiting cab, happy to escape his confinements, albeit for a short time. By the time we had reached the 'Big Top' of Clarke's Circus, Holmes's researches were evidently already well under way. He was dusting off his trousers in a disgruntled manner and Lestrade was standing nearby, wearing an air of triumphant smugness.

When I entered the Walker's changing room, alongside my canine companion, Lestrade could not contain his derisory laughter.

'Oh, Mr Holmes! I simply cannot imagine what assistance you expect to obtain from this poor bedraggled creature!' Poor Carlton Clarke, who was standing within earshot, looked forlorn and crestfallen.

Undaunted, Holmes replied: 'We shall see, we shall see, but Toby has yet to fail me.' Holmes greeted the dog with a vigorous rubbing of its head. 'Now, Mr Clarke, is there anything that you see in the room, which you would immediately associate with the missing Labrador?' he continued cheerily.

While Clarke conducted his own search Holmes identified to me the various points of interest that he had observed within the room. There was none that I could associate with the innocence of the now incarcerated knife-thrower, although I was fascinated by the patterns drawn by the knife marks that decorated a large wooden board. The unerring accuracy of each of Walker's throws was awesome to behold and the precise outline of a female body was there for all to see.

'Surely those marks alone confirm the guilt of Alfred Walker. Someone capable of such consistent accuracy would hardly miss the mark so dramatically,' Lestrade sneered, having observed our interest in the marks.

'Neither would he be the fool that you make him out to be,' Holmes responded. 'It is inconceivable that a man of his reputation would bring about his wife's demise in such a clumsy and obvious manner. No, Lestrade, there must be another explanation. There has to be. Now, Mr Clarke, did the Walkers go through the same routine every time they rehearsed?'

'Oh, absolutely. Each rehearsal was a private performance of the act.'

'Were the knives thrown in the same order every time?'

'Every time,' Clarke confirmed. 'The first knife thrown was always the one above the head.'

'Note that, Watson, the fatal knife was the first and only one thrown that night!'

'What are you driving at, Mr Holmes?' Lestrade enquired anxiously.

'Were the blindfolds always employed in rehearsals?' Holmes next asked, ignoring Lestrade's question.

'With all due respect, Mr Holmes, there would be no point otherwise,' Clarke replied, clearly as confused at Holmes's line of questioning as the rest of us.

'Therefore, if Sonia Walker had altered her stance or positioning that evening Alfred could not possibly have been aware of it,' Holmes murmured to himself.

'But Holmes, Sonia would hardly have deliberately jeopardized her own life by doing so,' I suggested.

'Quite so. Unless she was not …' Holmes's words trailed off with his thoughts, which for the time being remained his own. Yet, strangely, I now felt renewed confidence in his ability to clear Alfred Walker.

'So, Mr Clarke, there is nothing in the room that might aid Toby in his search?' Holmes asked, having recovered his composure.

'Sadly not.' The circus owner shook his head slowly and the smirk on Lestrade's face broadened visibly.

Holmes snatched Toby's leash from my grasp.

'Gentlemen, I suggest we meet again at Baker Street this evening. Come, Watson, the instincts of our canine friend here may yet prove to be more reliable than those of certain humans that I might care to mention!'

Once we were out of earshot of the others and with Toby not pursuing any obvious trail, I quietly broached a subject that I had feared might prove to be a delicate one.

'Holmes, in the absence of a scent for him to pursue, surely Toby's presence here is now redundant.'

Surprisingly, under the circumstances, an enigmatic smile slowly lit up Holmes's face. 'On the contrary, it is more valuable than before. See here.' Slowly Holmes extracted a sliver of what appeared to be red leather from his waistcoat pocket. 'You see, Watson, they searched yet they did not observe. If I am not mistaken I hold here the only remnant that Goldie left behind of Sonia Walker's red shoes.' He held this directly beneath Toby's dripping nose and at once the beast began to stir.

He took a few sniffs with no obvious purpose or urgency at first, but slowly the momentum increased and in a short while Holmes and I were being led from tent to tent and caravan to caravan throughout the circus encampment. Once or twice we startled various artistes as they prepared for their acts, their astonished screams and shrills adding to the mayhem of our urgent progress. However there was still no sign of our golden quarry.

In the end, and to our consternation, Toby led us beyond the confines of the circus and on to a stretch of wasteland just beyond.

'Do not be concerned, Watson, this, I am certain is where Walker exercised his dog. Toby will lead us to our goal in no time,' Holmes encouraged me breathlessly.

For a few agonizing minutes it appeared that, for once, Holmes was sadly mistaken. Toby's movements became hesitant and all seemed to be lost as he stopped dead in his tracks and lay down. Undeterred, Holmes waved the strip of leather under Toby's nose once more and in an instant he was up on his feet again, frantically sniffing the ground around him.

'Quickly, Watson! He would seem to be leading us towards that hollow over there.'

The ground that we had been traversing so far, had been flat and almost bare of vegetation, apart from the occasional berry bush and the odd stunted tree. Just in front of us, however, a lushly wooded dell was suddenly revealed to us. With some difficulty we scrambled down its steep stony slope and when we collapsed on to the floor at its base Toby broke away from Holmes's grasp of his leash and disappeared into the tangle of the undergrowth.

The determination of Toby's sudden surge forward seemed to indicate that he was now certain of his quarry. We floundered in his wake, but were unable to match his speed and lost sight of him altogether. We feared that he had disappeared for good and that he had gone off on a wild-goose chase when, all of a sudden his distinctive bark echoed through the trees from just a few yards ahead of us.

Toby was clearly pleased with himself, for he came bounding over to us with his tail flailing about wildly. He led us towards a large hollow that had formed, over the years, at the base of an immense oak. While I regained Toby's leash Holmes dropped to the ground and crawled towards this depression on his stomach. He was greeted by a terrible snarling and a hostile display of teeth that were most uncharacteristic of a Labrador.

Holmes employed the same soothing tones that had so often quelled the fears of some of our more distraught female clients and in a moment or two he had successfully coaxed the dog from his lair. He then called for me to join him on the ground. Having secured both dogs to a tree I did his bidding.

'See here Watson. Was there ever a more convincing display of a dog's devotion to his master than this?'

I stared into the darkness, to where Holmes indicated, yet all that I could see was a strange collection of mangled pieces of red leather within the darkest recesses of the tree-trunk.

'I don't understand,' I protested. 'There is nothing here that would indicate devotion.'

'Very likely not, yet this display, described by Carlton Clarke as the dog's "peculiar penchant" is nothing of the sort! He is destroying the most prized possessions that once belonged to the object of his hate and the cause of his abject misery. However, there is much more of relevance to be learnt here than merely the understanding of the wretchedness of a dog.'

Before I could question him as to the exact significance of this latest discovery he sprang to his feet and made a small sack out of his jacket by tying its sleeves together in a tight knot. Into this bundle he now threw the remnants of leather that he had gathered from the base of the oak. He next improvised a leash from his necktie with which he successfully secured the Labrador.

'Watson, please return our trusty ally to Pinchin Lane. I shall make one last enquiry before rejoining you and our client at Baker Street.' Without another word Holmes turned and began making his way up the side of the dell with the reluctant Goldie in tow.

Toby proved to be more reluctant to return to his cage in Sherman's menagerie than he had been to escape it. None the less, I was still able to return to our rooms before either Lestrade or Carlton Clarke and, most surprisingly it appeared, Sherlock Holmes. That mystery was solved a moment later, though, when his voice rang out from behind his bedroom door.

'A thousand apologies, Watson, yet, as you have observed, I had need to replace almost half of my wardrobe!' He laughed.

A moment later he bounded into the room and immediately offered me a Cognac and one of his favourite Indian cigars.

'The satisfactory conclusion to a most unusual and problematic case is cause for a small celebration, would you not say?' He smiled while applying the flame of a vesta to the tip of my cigar.

'I could reply more definitively if I was to be more enlightened as to the exact details of its conclusion.' I responded through a column of dark and resinous smoke.

'Quite so and yet, unless I am very much mistaken, the time of your enlightenment is not too far away.' Holmes was glancing casually through the window and I correctly concluded that our two guests had just arrived at our door. Once our guests had returned to the chairs they had occupied before, Holmes extinguished his cigar and filled his cherry-wood from the Persian slipper as a prelude to his dénouement of the case. However it was Lestrade who spoke first.

'I assume, Mr Holmes, that you have summoned us here to offer your sincere apologies to both the disillusioned Mr Clarke and myself.' He said, still retaining his air of pugnacious confidence.

'I was certain that this would prove to be your inevitable and yet erroneous conclusion, Mr Lestrade!' Holmes responded whilst intentionally and maliciously omitting the hapless detective's correct title. 'You have careered clumsily through this case, basing all of your conclusions upon the evidence thrust into your face, without once standing back to analyse it.

'Would a man possessing the talents and intellect with which Alfred Walker was so obviously endowed, commit a deliberate murder in so clumsy a manner? His heartrending display of grief, at the side of his wife's corpse, and his intention to give his valued and faithful dog away, merely to appease her, were hardly the acts of a man set upon taking the life of his wife and partner. Mr Clarke, here, has attested to Walker's enduring love and devotion in the face of almost intolerable abuse, and he was a model professional to the last.'

Lestrade now visibly reddened and began to shift uncomfortably in his seat.

'Yet what other conclusion is one supposed to draw when faced with these incontrovertible facts?' he asked in more subdued tones than he had used at first.

'Broaden your field of vision, Inspector and make use of your limited imagination! Once we have concluded that Sonia's death was not as a result of a malicious act, the only solution is that her demise was a tragic accident, although the cause of this is less obvious, given the uncanny accuracy of Walker's throwing prowess.

'Watson knows my methods and the first action I took was to conduct a thorough examination of the floor of the room in which the incident took place. More especially, the direction of my enquiry took in to account, to some degree, the strange behaviour of Goldie the Labrador. After all, Labradors, as a rule, are quiet and docile animals and not prone to erratic behaviour. Once my questioning had established the exact routine and circumstances of the rehearsals, I realized at once that Walker was surely as much surprised at the tragic outcome on this occasion as everybody else had been and that the flight of his faithful hound had been of secondary importance to him.

'I then discovered a small scrap of mangled red leather, in a corner of the room and duly noted the complete absence of any other traces of the distinctive red shoes. Thereupon my decision to send for Toby appeared to have been vindicated, despite your own reservations, Inspector.'

'So far I have not heard anything to dispel those reservations,' Lestrade replied, some confidence returning to his manner.

In reply Holmes turned on his heel and a moment later returned from his room bearing his makeshift sack. He untied the sleeves and allowed its strange contents to cascade on to the floor at his feet. Lestrade laughed uproariously and gleefully clapped his hands.

'Oh, Mr Holmes, you have surpassed yourself this time! What tomfoolery is this?!' he cried, whilst the crestfallen Carlton Clarke turned ruefully away.

'This idiocy of mine,' Holmes declared, with bitter irony, 'will, undoubtedly restore Alfred Walker to his rightful place, in the centre of the ring at Clarke and Clarke's Circus!'

'Why, these are nothing more than mangled shreds!' Clarke cried in despair.

'At first glance they undoubtedly are, but they also hold the key to Walker's innocence. Goldie's devotion to his master was such that he felt compelled to destroy the most valued possession of his tormentor. These are the remains of Sonia's most treasured shoes. Yet, on closer examination, one realizes that there are two pairs of shoes amongst this débris, one pair far newer than the other.'

'How can you possibly tell which is which?' Lestrade asked, no longer feigning any indifference.

Holmes beckoned for Lestrade to join him on the floor. Slowly picking out certain pieces of leather from the rest, Holmes painstakingly reconstructed the crude outline of a left shoe. 'See how the manufacturer's mark has been almost obliterated by constant use on this one. One moment, please.' While Holmes continued to piece together further bits of leather, Lestrade looked up to me for consolation as he watched his case collapsing before his eyes. He was to get none. Meanwhile Clarke's mood visibly lightened as he, too, dropped to his knees.

Holmes offered another partial reconstruction for them to examine. 'Now observe the condition of the label on this example.'

'Why, this shoe is almost brand-new!' Carlton Clarke exclaimed.

'It is brand-new,' Holmes corrected. 'On my way back to Baker Street, I called in on the vendors and they were able to confirm that this particular shoe, an unusually expensive pair, I might add, had only been available since last week. Apparently they are this season's latest fashion and are distinguished from last season's collection by one vital detail. See here, the heel is a full inch higher than that of the old pair!'

'Good heavens, Mr Holmes! This is too marvellous. I cannot believe that I doubted you, even for one moment,' Clarke cried.

Ignoring this display Holmes continued: 'I am certain that Walker was not aware of his wife's fancy for the latest fashion, and would, therefore have made no allowance for her change in height. Equally, the shop assistant was convinced that Sonia Walker's obsessive desire to obtain this stylish footwear would have blinded her to its potential dangers. A simple measurement from the top of her head will, without doubt, confirm the tragic consequences of this lack of awareness.'

Lestrade slowly laboured back to his seat and wiped his brow as he sank down.

'Mr Holmes, once again you have saved an innocent man from the gallows, using the most unlikely of means. I will set the wheels in motion as soon as I return to the Yard.'

'For my part, I shall ensure that your name resounds throughout the length and breadth of the whole country!' Clarke proclaimed.

Holmes laughed at this. 'I can assure you, Mr Clarke, that my name has already resounded enough for my liking, thanks to my chronicler here. So I would thank you if my part in this affair remains anonymous.

'Besides which, my fleeting visit to Scotland Yard showed me that it was your faith in the man's character that proved to be his salvation. I was fortunate in gaining access to Walker's cell and his version of the events that you described to me, confirmed every facet of the case. Certainly, Mr Clarke, you are as fine a judge of human nature as you are a raconteur!'

As I placed my pencil down upon the table, I could not help but smile at my friend's humility.

'That is indeed most gracious of you, Mr Holmes, under the circumstances,' Lestrade quietly acknowledged.

As the two men slowly made their way towards the door Holmes suddenly called them back.

'Oh Lestrade, there is one small service that you can perform for me.'

Holmes returned to his bedroom once more and this time he re-emerged with Goldie still tethered to his necktie. 'Be sure to return this fine beast to its rightful owner, upon his release!'

THE ADVENTURE OF THE
CUTTER *ALICIA*

'... No less remarkable is that of the cutter Alicia, *which sailed one spring morning into a small patch of mist from which she never again emerged ...'*

(*The Problem of Thor Bridge*, by A Conan Doyle)

The late spring and early summer of 1895 were made particularly noteworthy by virtue of the profusion of stimulating and challenging cases with which my friend, Sherlock Holmes, had been recently inundated. The climax of this golden period had been Holmes's apprehension of the notorious strangler, Peabody, whose reign of terror had led the regular constabulary to despair. Only Holmes's remarkable deduction, that the perpetrator of this series of odious murders would have no more than three fingers on his left hand, prevented Peabody from eluding their inept grasp once again.

By way of a celebration of this latest triumph of his, Holmes suggested an evening attending a violin recital by the esteemed Russian maestro, Leshtikov, culminating with a lavish feast at Marcinis. I could not have been more delighted at these arrangements and not one aspect of the evening failed to live up to our expectations. I had rarely seen my friend more relaxed and at peace with the world, and as for myself, seldom have I felt fuller and more content after a meal. With this in mind, I suggested that we forgo the luxury of a cab for our homeward journey and instead negotiate the two or three miles on foot. Holmes thought this would be an excellent means of aiding our digestion and so, after hurling our half-smoked cigars towards the kerbside, we struck off briskly towards Baker Street.

To begin with, our walk was pleasant enough and, as we slowed our pace, Holmes launched into a most enlightening discourse upon the subject of Leshtikov's fingering and interpretation. When, however, he suddenly broke off in mid sentence, I glanced towards him and was immediately struck by a dramatic alteration in his countenance. His eyes blazed with excitement and his hitherto relaxed features were tightened in concentration. He pressed his lips with his left forefinger and whispered through them:

'Do not alarm yourself, old fellow, neither should you turn round just now or alter your gait, but I do believe that we are being followed. Rather clumsily and amateurishly, I will admit, so I am certain that we are not in any immediate danger, but please, nevertheless, when the moment is right, follow my lead.'

'This is outrageous!' I protested, in equally muted tones. 'Are you certain of this? I had not noticed anything untoward.'

'Really, Watson, you surprise me. They are not exactly expert at this.'

'There is more than one of them?'

'Two to be precise, a man and a woman. The man is of above average height, slim of build and probably in his twenties. The woman is considerably shorter, of similar age and slightly asthmatic.'

'Come now, Holmes, you cannot possibly know all this. I have closely attended your every word during the past ten minutes, and you have not once turned your head either to the right or the left!'

'Watson, there is more to the art of observation than using your eyes. Whilst you have been hanging on my every word, I have been listening to our pursuers' inept attempts to match the rhythm of their footsteps to our own. The constant alterations and hesitations that they have made throughout are what first alerted me to their attendance. As to their height and gender, the timbre of a young lady's shoes is always more clipped and less resonant by virtue of their raised and narrower heels. The man has had little difficulty in matching our speed and stride pattern; therefore I deduce that he is of a similar height to our own. The young lady, on the other hand, has had to apply almost twice as many strides as her companion, in maintaining our speed, resulting in a breathlessness one would not normally expect in an otherwise healthy woman of her age. But see here … an unprotected doorway!'

As we turned a corner, Holmes grabbed my jacket sleeve and manoeuvred me into the recessed entrance of a small furniture shop. 'They will panic as they turn the corner and find that we have disappeared from view. As they rush past us we shall accost them from behind.' Observing me vainly rummaging in my jacket pockets, Holmes added: 'Do not regret the absence of your revolver, Watson, I am certain that my loaded cane handle will more than suffice for these two.'

We waited silently and breathlessly within the confines

of the doorway for a moment or two when, sure enough, the otherwise deserted pavement, gave up the sound of two sets of footsteps coming to a halt at the very corner from which we had just turned. They quickened as they approached us, I could now distinguish the long strides of the man's steps and the clip of the young woman's heels as they sought to take up our trail. Holmes shot me a knowing smile as I acknowledged my recognition of this.

As soon as the couple had hurried past us we gave up our hiding-place and stealthily approached them from behind. As we drew closer Holmes placed his hand on the young man's right shoulder while I did likewise to the woman's left. Neither offered any form of resistance and they both turned around slowly, their faces riddled with fear and guilt.

'Oh Mr Holmes!' The woman exclaimed. 'Please do not have us arrested. We meant no harm. We simply did not know how to approach so esteemed a gentleman as yourself. Your recent clients have included royalty and the like and our problem seems so insignificant by comparison.'

'My dear lady, you must calm yourself,' Holmes responded, at his gentlest and most charming. 'No one is going to have you arrested. However, judging by your brother's silence and dour countenance I would say that he disapproves of your approaching me a good deal more than I do myself.'

The young man flushed with embarrassment. 'It is not that so much, sir, and I mean no disrespect, but I do believe that the matter of one's father's sanity is not a subject one should discuss with strangers.'

'Your father's sanity? Well, Watson, this may be a subject upon which you will have more knowledge than I. Young lady, I really do not see what possible assistance I can render you in this matter.' With that Holmes turned away and resumed his walk towards Baker Street.

'A moment, please sir,' The young lady's voice pierced the silent night air and caused Holmes to pause in his tracks, but not to turn. 'My father's sanity is not the issue here, more the authenticity of what he claims to have witnessed.' At this, Holmes slowly turned and began retracing his steps.

'He claims to have observed the *Alicia* on her fateful voyage!' Holmes concluded his return to us at a sprint.

'Our rooms are but a five minutes' walk from here!' With a dramatic flourish, Holmes waved them to walk ahead of us.

It had been Holmes's intention to follow the young couple all the way to our rooms, however his enthusiasm and impatience overcame any such restraint. Consequently he led the way, almost at a sprint; the couple tried to match his pace whilst I brought up the rear to ensure that they concluded their journey.

By the time the young couple and I eventually arrived at 221b, a somewhat bleary-eyed and dishevelled Mrs Hudson had already been coerced into preparing a tray of coffee. We also discovered that Holmes had, absent-mindedly, discarded his coat on the stairs in his haste to ascend them. I retrieved it as we made our way up and found Holmes pacing the room with his pipe already alight.

'A thousand apologies, Mrs Hudson, for causing a distur-bance at such an hour, but the matter is of the utmost moment,' Holmes declared, as he took the tray from her unsteady grasp. He then ushered her out once more, some-what unceremoniously, by way of a gentle shove upon her shoulders.

'Well I must say—' Mrs Hudson began to protest.

'Goodnight, Mrs Hudson!' Holmes called, once the door had been slammed shut behind her. I smiled apologetically towards the young couple when I observed their embarrassed exchange of glances, to which, I might add, Holmes was totally oblivious.

I invited our guests to share the sofa, upon which they perched themselves uncomfortably, whilst I picked up my notebook and pencil. Holmes returned his pipe to the mantelpiece temporarily before turning to face them.

The young lady spoke first:

'I apologize for my brother's earlier apparent brusqueness, but the embarrassment that we both feel is harder for a man to suppress, with his stronger inherent sense of family pride.'

Holmes waved this aside with the briefest of smiles.

'Do not concern yourself with the niceties at such a time. The national newspapers have kept Dr Watson and myself well enough informed with regard to the tragic and mysterious loss of the *Alicia* and for your father to claim to have witnessed this calamity is more than enough for you to bear. Unfortunately the authorities have not seen fit to involve us at this time, so for you to engage us would be something of a feather in our cap and a means to prise open the door that, hitherto, has been closed to us.'

'It is indeed strange that you have not been consulted upon this matter, Mr Holmes, but please let me explain our involvement and predicament in the hope that both your mystery and ours might yet be solved,' the young lady offered.

'That is indeed an excellent idea, for apart from the obvious facts that you are both from Leigh-on-Sea, in Essex, and that someone very close to you, though patently not your brother, is a seafaring man, I know nothing of you whatsoever! Perhaps you might begin by furnishing Dr Watson and his notebook with your names.'

'Why yes, of course. It is most reprehensible of me not to have done so this far. I am Mildred Lomas and this is my brother Edward.' Miss Lomas said these words slowly, clearly bemused at the accuracy of Holmes's observations.

'Do not look so amazed, Miss Lomas. As the good doctor here will testify, there is nothing miraculous in what I do, only observation, deduction and pure logic. For example, I have yet to encounter a sailor who has not badly scored the insides of his hands with the scars of the ship rope on which he is constantly pulling. Your brother's palms are as blemish free as on the day he was born. Furthermore, the exquisitely carved shark's tooth that you wear around your neck as a pendant is an example of work only undertaken by a man of the sea. The fact that this sailor is close to you can be attested to by the quality of the work that has affixed the pendant to the chain. With no disrespect intended, this clearly belies the quality and condition of your other apparel and is, therefore, of great importance to you and was no doubt, a gift from your father. Identifying your home was simplicity itself. The splashes of mud, on both of your boots, are of a colour and consistency unique to the upper reaches of the Thames estuary. No other town along that stretch of the Essex coast can boast of a mooring large enough to accommodate the type of vessel capable of reaching the depths wherein a tooth of that size might be found.' Without waiting for a reaction to his astounding explanation, Holmes suddenly turned away and reclaimed his pipe, which he promptly relit.

'Mr Holmes, I now understand why my sister was so eager to seek your help,' Edward Lomas stated gravely. Without acknowledging this remark Holmes promptly asked: 'Since you appear to be more anxious to air your thoughts than your brother, Miss Lomas, I should be obliged if you would explain your exact connection with the affair of the missing cutter and why you fear for the sanity of your father.'

'I will certainly do my best, Mr Holmes,' Miss Lomas replied. Before beginning her story she took a long grateful sip of her coffee. Her pale cheeks suddenly started to redden with suppressed emotion as she began her narrative.

'The *Alicia* was the last of the full-rigged cutters ever to set sail out of the harbour at Leigh. As such she commanded a certain sentimental respect from all who worked at the yard. Every time she put out of harbour, old sailors sitting on the boards, repairing their nets and tackle, would put down their work, for a moment, doff their caps or wave their scarves as she majestically glided by. I mention this, Mr Holmes,' Miss Lomas clearly sensed Holmes's growing impatience, 'because no number of newspaper articles can do full justice to the great sense of deprivation felt by the whole community at the loss of the *Alicia*.

'I am quite certain that this popular demonstration of grief has been a contributing factor behind the maltreatment and incarceration of our father. Men who have known my father well over many years have, seemingly, turned against him and even participated in the heckling and ridicule of him on the day that he was led away.' Miss Lomas was barely able to complete the sentence before she gave way to her emotions and began sobbing uncontrollably.

Despite the gentleness of his earlier treatment of Miss

Lomas, Holmes now found it quite impossible to cope with her tearful display of grief. Consequently he waved me, distractedly, towards the stricken woman and I was successful in stilling her by administering hot coffee while her brother applied soft soothing strokes to her forehead with a dampened sponge. After repeatedly blowing her nose and then apologizing profusely, Miss Lomas felt ready to continue with her remarkable tale.

'Mr Holmes, in view of the tendency that the popular press has towards distortion and embellishment, I think it best that I lay before you the bare facts pertaining to the loss of the *Alicia*, as they are understood by the local people. You will then better understand why our father's somewhat differing interpretation of events has caused such a furore within the community.' Holmes smiled and nodded his affirmation.

'Because of her age and yet despite confirmation of her continued seaworthiness, the *Alicia*'s range had been reduced in recent years, to cross-channel runs and occasional excursions to northern Spain. Her last voyage, as it subsequently proved to be, was to have been one of the former. She was carrying a cargo of coke, oil and twine and a small crew mastered by Captain Johnson, a man well used to piloting those waters. The weather was set fair, so a larger crowd than was usual congregated to watch her negotiate the estuary until she disappeared from view and out into the open sea.

'Mr Holmes, we thought nothing more of her until word came, from Dieppe, that the *Alicia* had not arrived, in accordance with her appointed schedule. This was inexplicable to us. There had been no wind to speak of, that might have blown her off course. The vessel and her company had made this very journey a thousand times before! There would have been no rocks or other obstacles that she might have encountered along her route; indeed, the size of her hull and the brevity of the voyage would have meant that she would have to have been shipping water not long after leaving harbour for her to have sunk in mid-channel.

'Consequently, the only reasonable explanation for her inexplicable loss was a collision with another vessel. The recent inclement weather had led to patches of grey mist floating haphazardly over the Channel. Collisions in these conditions are not unknown although, mercifully, quite rare. Therefore the owner of the vessel, Mr Nathaniel Garside, a successful local businessman and communal benefactor, dispatched a small flotilla of local craft with instructions to search along the *Alicia*'s projected course for traces of wreckage and, the Lord willing, to pick up any survivors. The harbour master at Dieppe dispatched a similar group of craft on the same mission, in fact some craft even converged upon the same mid-Channel location, but, despite all their efforts, all boats returned to their respective ports in empty-handed despair. After this operation was repeated on the following day, with the same unfortunate result, all hope was deemed to be lost. Mr Garside was left distraught at the loss of his vessel and the families of the crew members were rendered inconsolable.

'The loss of the *Alicia* appeared destined to become logged amongst one of the great unsolved nautical mysteries until my father decided to speak up.'

All this while Holmes had been sitting with his eyes tight shut in a state of intense concentration. He said not a word and moved not a muscle and so bizarre was his appearance that Miss Lomas was prompted to pause for a moment,

raising a questioning glance in my direction, as to whether
Holmes was even awake. Holmes answered her doubts
himself by suddenly jumping up from his chair and
fumbling for a match with which to relight his pipe.

'Miss Lomas,' he began, 'I must congratulate you. To a
man as ignorant as myself of nautical matters, your narrative has proved both informative and stimulating. However,
to a student of all that is extraordinary and, seemingly,
unsolvable your tale is both gratifying and tantalizing. On
the surface, the events and circumstances that you have
described are impossible to accept. Therefore I must urge
you to describe to me your unfortunate father's version of
what took place.'

'Mr Holmes, I do not seek either your congratulations or
your gratification.' Miss Lomas's cheeks were flushed as she
admonished Holmes for his strange vocabulary. 'However
you refer to my father as "unfortunate" which seems to indicate that you already regard him as a victim of injustice.
This fills me with fresh hope.'

'My dear young lady, you must not take offence at my
poor use of the English language. Equally, it would be
unwise to build up what may prove to be false hopes at this
early stage. Let us just say that I will not prejudge anything
that you tell me until I am in full possession of the facts.'
Holmes smiled as he waved her to continue.

All this while Edward Lomas had been sitting in passive
silence, upright with both hands flat upon his knees. He
now placed his arm comfortingly about his sister's shoulder.
When he spoke it was with a strong, educated tone that
belied his youthful, fresh-faced countenance.

'Mr Holmes, my dearest Mildred, I think it best that I
continue with the remainder of our story. My sister might

find it difficult to contain her emotions as we must inevitably touch upon an unfortunate weakness in our father's nature.' Miss Lomas smiled gratefully at her brother and nodded her agreement to his suggestion.

Edward Lomas betrayed his discomfiture by repeatedly clearing his throat. Holmes offered him a cigarette, which Lomas gratefully accepted.

'Well, gentlemen, there is no point in beating around the bush. In common with many men of the sea our father has a fondness for rum that manifests itself when he is landbound for any length of time. However his penchant for the camaraderie of the local inns often precludes all else and it has cost him many a lucrative voyage, of late. When he remains indoors he is an intelligent and kindly man and a good and loving father. I should mention also that we lost our poor mother some years ago to the tuberculosis. When once at his cups, however, it is impossible to persuade him to come home and he will spend most of his time and what little money he might have on rum for himself and his old shipmates, who take advantage of his misguided generosity and ridicule him for his jovial nature. He is now more renowned for his singing and amusing tales than ever he was for his abilities aboard ship.

'Gentlemen, it is precisely because of his reputation as a "rummy" that his claim to have witnessed the last moments of the *Alicia* before she was lost was never taken seriously. Night after night he would repeat his tale to whoever he could find to listen to him. These persons, however, became progressively fewer, and soon folk began to find his assertions offensive rather than amusing. Those who had lost loved ones when the *Alicia* went down, employees of Mr Garside, even strangers who knew nothing of him, began clamouring to have him removed from the various taverns he was accustomed to frequent. Eventually he resorted to drinking alone at home and at least there, Mildred and I might enjoy some success in weaning him from his poison.'

At this point I paused from my frantic taking of notes and raised my hand to stop Lomas in mid-narrative.

'Forgive my interruption, Mr Lomas, but I do not understand how your father's addiction to alcohol could possibly lead to his incarceration on the grounds of insanity. Indeed, would not his reputation for drinking have saved him from such a fate? Surely his assertions, which everyone seemed to find so strange and offensive, would have been put down to rum rather than brain fever?' I suggested, whilst noting Holmes's look of surprised admiration at my timely interruption.

'Indeed, Dr Watson, and that surely would have been the case were it not for the fact that he continued to make these claims even after our success in sobering him. In fact he began to restate his claims with increased insistence and detail, and began to force these upon the local authorities. He became something more than just the local nuisance and once the police became involved it was only a matter of time before action was taken against him. When he was brought before the local assizes we implored him to desist from these claims of his, but he was insistent and was still yelling them out up to the moment when he was forcibly removed. The last time we saw him he implored that my sister and I, at least, should believe in him. He was locked away in the knowledge that we did and, indeed still do. Now we ask that you help us to clear his name.'

'I can make no such promise at this stage,' Holmes replied. 'However, if you inform me, as exactly as you can, of the claim your father is making, together with the name of the arresting officer, I promise to be on the first available train to Leigh-on-Sea with that express intention, I hope with my friend and colleague Dr Watson in close attendance.'

'I should be honoured,' I answered in reply to the three expectant glances cast towards me.

'Thank you, gentlemen,' Lomas said with much relief, whereupon Holmes passed him another cigarette.

'Our father was returning from a night's fishing trip aboard a small sailing dinghy he used from time to time. On this occasion he was after some dab for our Friday supper and having had little success within the estuary, found himself drifting out towards the open sea. From these depths he pulled out a substantial haul, enough for our supper and leaving him with a surplus to sell on the quayside. By the time that he turned for home it was almost dawn and he was celebrating his catch by way of a small flask containing rum. In the distance he saw a familiar shape moving in the opposite direction. It was, of course, the *Alicia*. He saluted her by raising his flask aloft, then, remembering how small was the cargo she was supposed to have been carrying, was immediately struck by how low in the water she was sitting.'

Holmes made a gesture towards my notebook. 'Note that well, Watson; it is, I am sure, of the utmost significance.' Then he waved towards Lomas to continue.

'Our father, full of curiosity, promptly turned about and continued watching the *Alicia*'s progress out into the North Sea. This he was only able to do for a short while, because every so often patches of mist drifted across her course. One such patch of mist appeared on the *Alicia*'s port side, a patch notable for its large size and density and, to our father's amazement the *Alicia* suddenly changed course and began tacking directly towards it!

'Within a few minutes she was completely engulfed. Our father sat there, transfixed by this most singular navigational decision, and awaited the *Alicia*'s emergence at the mist's furthest extremity, which was clearly in his field of vision. Based on her previous rate of knots, he expected this to occur within but a few moments. However, he sat there eagerly consuming his rum for close to half an hour, before realizing, in a state of great agitation, that she must have met with disaster. For she never appeared from the far side of that mist!

'It was inconceivable that she could have brought herself to a halt within such a short distance. It was equally improbable that she was a victim of a collision, those waters are particularly well charted and have long been deemed as safe from all manner of obstacles. Any second vessel would have been clearly visible, from our father's vantage point, before having entered the mist from its opposite side. The only remaining explanation was that the hull had been accidentally holed, at a time prior to the *Alicia*'s encounter with the mist. Yet such was the shape and depth of her hull, for her to have sunk so close to harbour would have meant her being holed before setting off from Leigh. No captain with Richard Johnson's experience would have allowed that to happen. You see the whole thing is impossible!!' Lomas suddenly and violently exclaimed. He paused for a moment while he calmed himself by taking deep breaths.

'I apologize, gentlemen, for my unseemly outburst, but you see, when put like that, my father's claims do seem to verge towards the fanciful. The accepted version of events, that the *Alicia* met with a mid-channel collision, is the only one that makes any sense and yet—'

'Yet you find yourself believing your father, and I shall begin my investigation based on the premise that he was speaking the absolute truth. What action did he take next?' Holmes asked in his most calming of tones.

'Bless you, Mr Holmes, for believing in our poor father, although I would not have wondered had you not. Our father now reset his sail and turned his small craft about, towards the *Alicia*'s last visible position. He had hoped to pick up any survivors, but there was none. No survivors and no bodies! Mr Holmes, there was not even the smallest piece of wreckage to be found. It was as if the ship had never even existed. A vessel of her size cannot just sink without cause or trace. Yet all he could find, despite his diligent efforts, was a small stretch of hauling rope with a most strangely frayed end.

'Distraught and defeated he set sail for home once more and having reached shore spent the next forty-eight hours drinking himself into a stupor. By the time he had emerged from this word had already been received from Dieppe, the search flotillas been dispatched and had returned empty-handed. As my sister has previously explained, by this time our father's version of events seemed like the ramblings of a drunken lunatic to the townsfolk, who were feeling such a grievous loss. Mr Holmes, there is nothing more that we can tell you. Can you give us any hope?' Lomas was now leaning forward expectantly.

'The case against your father certainly seems to be a strong one,' Holmes responded gravely. 'Although the local authorities seemed to be somewhat prejudiced in their refusal to accept the possibility that the *Alicia* had set sail with a hole in her hull. Assuming that this premise is correct, however, then your case is raised up to an entirely different level altogether! I am equally curious about a haul rope with a frayed end.' Then, almost talking to himself, Holmes continued quietly: 'Yes, it is most perplexing, unless ...'

'Unless what, Holmes?' I queried.

'Watson! Look at the time!' Holmes suddenly exclaimed, clapping his hands together excitedly. 'We cannot expect these young people to return to the Essex coast at such an hour. I insist that you both stay the night and we shall all journey to Leigh-on Sea together on tomorrow's first available train.'

'We could not possibly so impose upon you,' Lomas objected, having exchanged a glance with his sister.

'Nonsense! As Watson will assure you, we have endured far less comfortable sleeping arrangements than our own sitting room! I shall have Mrs Hudson make up your beds at once.'

There was not a further word of argument and whilst I was bundled on to the settee, to make way for Miss Lomas, Holmes was more than pleased to take to his favourite chair for the night and vacate his room for her brother. Although my army training allowed me to fall asleep even under the most trying of conditions, what sleep I did take was most fitful. I was disturbed to note that, on each occasion that I awoke, my friend was still seated upright smoking heavily from his pipe, clearly with no inclination to fall asleep himself. During one such moment I interrupted his deep meditation with a softly whispered question.

'Holmes, clearly you have already formulated a germ of a theory that would not have occurred to another living soul.

Whilst I would not expect you to divulge its nature to me at this early stage, I strongly feel that there is an ulterior motive behind your invitation to the Lomases other than mere hospitality. Would you not, at the least, explain to me what that might be?'

Holmes turned slowly towards me, eyeing me quizzically whilst arching one eyebrow. He removed the pipe from his lips before replying in a hushed tone that was barely audible.

'Your inclination towards cynicism is matched only by your faculty for deduction, friend Watson. However, it is true to say that I am positive that there are certain interested parties in Leigh whom I would much prefer not to have prior notice of our coming. Whilst I am sure the Lomases would not have divulged this fact mischievously, they are, none the less, simple folk who might, inadvertently, have compromised our element of surprise. Now, our Bradshaw indicates an early departure from Fenchurch Street, so I would advise you to sleep rather than indulge in premature speculation.' Without another word Holmes relit his pipe and returned to his previous pose, leaving me to lull myself back to sleep with the type of idle theorizing that he would have despised.

Our early arrival, at the station the following morning allowed us the time for a light breakfast that Holmes had not permitted us to take at Baker Street. Our young guests seemed somewhat the worse for wear, no doubt a consequence of their unexpected overnight stay and the draining experience of relating their heart-rending tale, so they were extremely glad of this refreshment. There was an anticipatory silence in our carriage throughout the relatively short journey and we had actually arrived at the picturesque fishing village before a single word was spoken.

'I shall rejoin you by this evening!' Holmes announced to our complete astonishment. He promptly jumped back on to the train just as it had begun to pull away from the platform.

The Lomases turned to me, dismayed and bemused by Holmes's unexpected and sudden departure.

'Does Mr Holmes not now wish to assist us?' Mildred Lomas breathlessly asked of me.

'I am sure that that is still his intention,' I answered emphatically. 'However, Mr Holmes works to his own methods and, even his most surprising actions will be vindicated by their results.' Despite this outward display of cheerful optimism, I harboured my own misgivings at Holmes's infuriatingly enigmatic behaviour. His purpose in remaining on the train was completely beyond me. Surely, I reasoned, the mystery and therefore our investigation began and ended in the delightful, though now tragic, fishing village of Leigh-on-Sea. I briefly studied the schedule of the remainder of our train's journey, which indicated stops at Chalkwell, Westcliff, Southend, Thorpe Bay and Shoeburyness, yet none of these places suggested anything of interest or significance. Like the Lomases, I was resigned to awaiting Holmes's return before we could be enlightened as to the purpose of his mysterious departure.

Apologetically, the Lomases recommended the Ship hotel to me, as being ideal accommodation for Holmes and myself. Their small household was much disturbed, at present, and they were, therefore, unable to reciprocate our hospitality of the previous night. I waved this apology aside and suggested that we should all meet again after supper, by which time I was certain that Holmes would have rejoined us. They promptly agreed to this arrangement and

I was left to trudge off towards the bottom of Leigh Hill where, I understood, our tavern might be found, still in possession of Holmes's abandoned bag.

Our rooms were spartan and charmless, although they afforded a view of the estuary and a pungent odour from its mud flats. After a brief conversation with our equally charmless landlord, whereby I discovered our mealtimes and the tavern's reputation for having harboured smugglers in the old days, I struck out for Hadleigh Castle, the ruins of which our train had taken us past just prior to pulling into the station.

My walk was somewhat arduous as the ruins were at the summit of a steep hill. When I eventually reached them I was disappointed to discover that a single crumbling wall was all that remained of this small Norman castle. I only stayed long enough to enjoy a pipe before returning to the tavern in time for an early supper and, I had hoped, some news from my friend.

Upon my arrival I was disappointed to learn from the landlord that he had not yet seen or heard from Holmes and that the preparation of our supper was somewhat behind schedule. Therefore I took myself into the deserted saloon and ordered a pint of ale from the aged bartender. This individual was delighted to learn that I was a doctor and then proceeded to describe to me his various complaints and ailments whilst I patiently sipped at my beer. I was at the point of despair when I was alerted to the familiar smell of strong shag tobacco and at last observed a column of thick smoke rising from behind the back of a high-winged leather chair.

'I was wondering how long it would take you to become aware of my presence!' Holmes laughed as I tentatively stole round the side of his chair. He waved me towards a chair opposite his own and another glass of beer awaiting me on the table before it.

'I see you could not wait for me to join you before beginning your libations,' Holmes observed as I placed my existing drink on the table next to the new one. 'However, our supper is still some way off so you should have time to enjoy them both.'

'Beer, supper, by all means, however, you must inform me at once of the reasons for and the results of your strange disappearance at the station this morning!' I insisted.

'I must apologize for that, dear fellow, but I suddenly realized, as we got off the train, that your solitary arrival would draw far less attention than the two of us together. Therefore I decided to continue my journey to the end of the line, which terminates at Shoeburyness. This destination was well suited to my purposes providing, as it does, the last view of the Thames before it flows out into the North Sea. As I stood on that promontory I realized at once that an interested observer would be in a most advantageous position to either confirm, or rebut Lomas's assertions.

'I therefore set about looking for this individual if, indeed, he even existed. To my disappointment and surprise, my enquiries at the local inn did little to enlighten me. However, walking along the promenade I came upon two grizzled old sailors whiling away an idle afternoon together. I fell into conversation with them, and, Watson, to my great satisfaction they both remembered having seen the *Alicia* navigating her final departure from the estuary, on the morning in question—' At that moment our excitable young client, Miss Lomas, came bustling into the room.

'Oh, Mr Holmes!' she said breathlessly and with much relief in her voice. 'My brother and I were so taken aback by your abrupt departure this morning that I did not, in all honesty, expect to see you sitting here this evening!'

'Calm yourself, Miss Lomas.' Holmes laughed gently. 'I apologize for any undue agitation that I may have caused you, but as my friend Watson here will attest, I have never been able to resist a touch of the dramatic. However, console yourself with the fact that my enquiries at Shoeburyness have provided our investigation with a most positive starting point. There is now a glimmer of light penetrating the gloom that has surrounded you.'

The young lady was so overwhelmed with joyous emotion that she ran towards Holmes, and would undoubtedly have embraced him were it not for his raised arms warding her off.

'I knew from the outset that you would save our father!' she exclaimed.

The look of consternation upon Holmes's face slowly disappeared as he gently pushed Miss Lomas away from him. 'My dear young lady, your assumptions and demonstrations of joy are, alas, somewhat premature at this early stage. I can only confirm that I will now proceed, confident in the belief that your father's story is the absolute truth. To convince the authorities of this, sufficiently to effect his release will be quite another matter.'

Miss Lomas managed to calm herself while I showed her to a chair at our table.

'Please explain, Mr Holmes, how you reached your conclusion regarding the truth of my father's version of events,' Miss Lomas asked.

'Your arrival was well-timed, for I was about to set this

before Watson, so you have now saved me the tiresome task of repeating myself.'

'Will your brother not be joining us?' I asked, with some surprise at his absence.

'Unfortunately his work for Mr Garside as clerk and rent-collector sometimes extends into the evening, but he sends his apologies and I will inform him of any outcome.'

'Now I understand. I was concerned that perhaps he was still harbouring some misgivings about taking us into your confidence. I take it that his employer is the same Nathaniel Garside who owned the *Alicia*?' I asked.

'The very same,' Miss Lomas replied. 'He has many tenants in the local vicinity and Edward helps him administer his estate, but please, Mr Holmes, you were about to explain the results of your visit to Shoeburyness.'

'Of course, of course, but first please indulge me by answering a question or two of my own.' At this point Holmes leant back thoughtfully in his chair whilst drawing deeply on his pipe. 'Miss Lomas, to your knowledge were any members of Johnson's crew tenants of Mr Garside?'

'I should be very surprised if that were not so. Mr Garside owns a line of small cottages close by the creek and most of their occupants are seamen and their families. However, I am sure that my brother would be able to confirm this.'

At this, Holmes suddenly sat upright once more, clearly agitated by Miss Lomas's suggestion. Then, having sensed Miss Lomas's consternation at this unexpected reaction, he forced a smile and said: 'I would much appreciate it if you could confirm this through another source. At this stage, I do not think it is in your father's best interests for Mr Garside to have any inkling as to my line of enquiry.'

'I am sure that my brother would not mention it to Mr

Garside were you to request him not to,' Miss Lomas responded defensively.

'Nevertheless!' Holmes insisted.

'Of course, Mr Holmes, if you feel it is absolutely necessary.'

Holmes then leant back once more and relit his pipe.

'Now to my encounter in Shoeburyness this afternoon, with two aged, but sharp-eyed seamen,' he began, clearly much relieved at Miss Lomas's acquiescence. 'I will not divulge the names of the two gentlemen in question, at their request, but suffice it to say their evidence will prove to be of the greatest importance. They are old acquaintances of your father and are most anxious to aid in his release. No doubt the authorities are unaware of their existence and, consequently, of the information that they can bring to bear. Therefore they will keep a low profile, but they have assured me of their full co-operation once the moment comes.

'On the morning of the *Alicia*'s inexplicable disappearance they were enjoying their pipes on the promenade, as is their wont. Not only were they able to confirm your father's observation, that the *Alicia* was sitting unusually low in the water, but they are also willing to swear, under oath, that she had already begun listing to one side. Obviously, the mist obscured the *Alicia*'s final descent beneath the waves, but they are equally certain that she must have been shipping water before she had even left the harbour.'

'Whilst I am much relieved at this vindication of my father's word, it is almost inconceivable that a seaman of Captain Johnson's experience would ever put to sea in command of a craft in such a condition,' Miss Lomas observed gravely.

'Yet three independent witnesses have now confirmed this to be the case. You see, we are no longer investigating the mysterious disappearance of a vessel and her crew, but are now delving into one of the deepest and darkest cases that we have yet encountered,' Holmes solemnly declared.

I could contain myself no longer. 'Holmes, surely you are not suggesting that Johnson would have deliberately sabotaged his own vessel and jeopardized the lives of his crew!'

'I can think of no other explanation that would fit the facts. However, there is still much that we need to learn before I can present this to the authorities. Miss Lomas, can you tell me who is leading the investigation?'

'Scotland Yard sent an Inspector Fowler, a most odious and unsympathetic man, who seems to get on quite well with Nathaniel Garside.'

'Ah, so you have already formed this judgement of him. Watson, surely you remember our old friend from our investigation into the Egyptian gargoyle?' Holmes asked me sardonically.

'I most certainly do!' I replied emphatically. 'He was both arrogant and uncooperative, yet you sent him packing with a resounding flea in his ear. I rather fancy he will be more willing to co-operate with us on this occasion.'

'We shall see. However, there is little more that we can achieve this evening. May I prevail upon you to make your own discreet enquiries as to the domestic circumstances of the missing crew members, Miss Lomas, while Watson and I will endeavour to be Inspector Fowler's first visitors in the morning.' With that Miss Lomas took her leave of us and we, in turn, retired shortly afterwards.

We spent an uncomfortable night, in our spartan and cheerless rooms, so that we experienced no real difficulty in meeting the unreasonably early breakfast time offered by our landlord. I, at any rate, was somewhat compensated for this by being served a brace of the freshest and most delicious kippers I had ever eaten. Holmes made do with a couple of cigarettes and the occasional sip from a cup of almost undrinkable coffee.

We arrived at the local constabulary on Elm Road at a little after nine o'clock, only to discover that Inspector Fowler had not yet surfaced from his hotel. We decided to wait, little realizing that it would be another hour before his arrival. When he did at last appear he seemed dishevelled and in a state of some agitation. When he noticed us in the corner of the waiting-room this agitation seemed to heighten somewhat.

He greeted us with no more than a sneer and gestured us toward his office with an unceremonious jerk of his head. By the time we had joined him there he was in the process of ordering himself a cup of black coffee. After glancing in our direction, however, he increased the order to three.

'I trust that the police beverage will prove to be less poisonous than the one we were subjected to this morning at breakfast, eh, Watson? So, Inspector Fowler, why has Scotland Yard sent its very finest, to this neck of the woods?' Holmes cheerily enquired.

Ignoring Holmes's question, Fowler said: 'I am a little surprised that the small matter of a lost ship should have lured the illustrious Sherlock Holmes from Baker Street; more than a little off your usual path. Besides, my business here is all but complete; you have wasted your time and your journey.'

'The Lomases do not seem to think so. Indeed they are most anxious for us to stay and help towards securing their father's release. Now, I am sure that the authorities have a good reason for keeping me ignorant of this affair, equally I am certain that you have your own motives, despite the successful conclusion to the matter of the Egyptian gargoyle. If we work together, though, I am sure we can bring about the release of an innocent man.'

'You are so certain of his innocence?' Fowler asked, raising one eyebrow quizzically.

'As certain as I am that you have no intention of leaving for London today!' Holmes replied.

'Ah, your marvellous theories, once again,' Fowler responded.

'What might appear to be theories to an untrained and chaotic mind, are, to the logical reasoner, nothing more than simple observations. For example, just one glance at your face and the results of the haphazard use of a blunt razor blade indicates to me that you have no intention of meeting your superiors today, nor, therefore, of leaving Leigh-on-Sea.' Holmes concluded.

'That is all very well,' Fowler responded with some bitterness. 'However, I see little reason to favour Lomas's drink-fuelled version of events over that of the redoubtable Nathaniel Garside. Surely a man of logic, such as yourself, must dismiss the idea of a ship, the size of the *Alicia*, disappearing in a patch of mist!'

Holmes sipped disdainfully from his coffee cup. 'Inspector Fowler, perhaps you would be better served if you cultivated the ability to isolate the source of your information from the absolute truth. The fact that the source is from the mouth of an elderly seaman with a bent towards drink has clearly prejudiced your judgement. I am certain that you would not be in such a hurry to depart for London, with your work incomplete, if you had met the two witnesses who are both willing and able to corroborate Lomas's story.'

At these words Fowler leant forward on his desk and now seemed to view Holmes without any of the disdain that he had been displaying so far.

'Mr Holmes,' Fowler replied. 'I must tell you that at the time of our earlier collaboration I viewed your involvement in the case with both scepticism and resentment. However, events and conversations with Inspector Lestrade, have since corrected that point of view. Equally, I am sure that a man of your unique talents and abilities considered me as nothing more than an inefficient oaf, stumbling around blindly in search of my own misguided view of the truth.'

Holmes shuffled uneasily in his chair, never comfortable when confronted with compliments, whilst Fowler continued:

'However, I must assure you that whatever my shortcomings might be as a detective, I am hard-working and diligent and, above all else, a believer in justice and the truth.'

Clearly moved, by Fowler's fervent declarations, Holmes bowed his head with a smile and said: 'I am most reassured to hear you say so, Inspector Fowler.'

'As to the matter at hand, I must admit that I have been harbouring my own misgivings as to the manner in which this case has been conducted, even before your arrival in Leigh.' Fowler stated bluntly.

'Ah! Now to the crux of the matter.' Holmes now abandoned his attempts to consume his coffee, lighting a cigarette instead whilst that familiar glint lit up his grey eyes once again. 'Exactly what has caused these feelings of misgiving?'

'To begin with, my presence here has seemed to be both superfluous and, indeed, unwanted. The searches for the *Alicia* were conducted prior to my arrival without, I might add, the involvement of the local coastguard, solely at the instigation and under the auspices of Nathaniel Garside. Any attempts I have made at extracting information from the local force have been met with obstructions and my superiors at the Yard have instructed me to tread softly and not to intrude upon the deep sense of loss felt by the whole community. The incarceration of Lomas seems to have been for precisely that reason alone, with only his immediate family raising any objection to this at all!

I could not contain myself for another moment. 'I simply do not understand! Is there nobody involved, other than the Lomases and yourself, who wants to discover the truth? Surely the families of the lost seamen want to know the true fate of the *Alicia*?!' I exclaimed.

'For many seamen the very nature of their work precludes the comforts of a traditional family life. In the case of the *Alicia*, neither Captain Johnson nor any of his small crew was married,' Fowler replied.

'That is most convenient,' Holmes mumbled quietly to himself. However, before either Fowler or myself could query Holmes's strange comment he slapped his palms down hard on the edge of Fowler's desk, then jumped suddenly to his feet and proclaimed; 'Gentlemen, we shall have to build this case for ourselves, in spite of any obstructions strewn in our path! Are you up for it Inspector, bearing in mind the detrimental effect it might have on your career?'

'I should be honoured, Mr Holmes. Just allow me time to shave, please, there was really no incentive whilst I was merely acting as the appearance of officialdom.' Holmes nodded his agreement.

'Then I propose a bracing walk by the harbour. Who knows what we might discover by the shore!'

Holmes and I waited enviously in the lobby of Fowler's hotel while he set urgently about his toilet. We discovered that the original building, the Peter Boat Inn had burnt to the ground in '92, whereupon it was revealed that its cellar had been used to store the contraband of local smugglers. The inn had been rebuilt as a most splendid hostelry which surely put ours to shame. Perhaps more significantly, we discovered that in the early part of the century, small cutters, otherwise known as 'Bawleys', had often been used by smugglers, when not engaged in their lawful employment of cockling.

Within a few minutes, a clean-shaven Inspector Fowler came bounding enthusiastically down the stairs towards us.

'By the way, Mr Holmes,' Fowler said hastily as we struck out towards the shoreline, 'at the time of Lomas's arrest, there was one dissenting voice, which I omitted to inform you of, namely Edward Burnley, otherwise known throughout the community as "Uncle Ted". However, I should warn you that his objection to Lomas's arrest could have had more to do with his opposition to Garside than his belief in Lomas's innocence.'

'Which aspect of Garside is Burnley so opposed to?' Holmes asked, strangely amused by the use of the word 'opposition'.

'Oh, the two gentlemen have been rivals for as long as anyone cares to remember. Between them they own and operate nearly every noteworthy business in the area.

Garside, for example, is the principal shareholder in the gas company and even instigated the installation of the street lighting. They are for ever running against each other for control of the parish council. However, in all respects, they are as unlike each other as you could ever expect two people to be. Whilst Garside is tall and austere, in his ridiculously high hats, Burnley is short and rotund with a full white beard and a penchant for checked caps and gold watch-chains. Even politically they are fierce opposites. Although held in great affection by the local electorate, Burnley is also regarded by many as being something of an eccentric for holding some of his most liberal opinions, which he is never shy of expressing at every opportunity.'

'Well,' I laughed, 'in some respects you certainly have not wasted your time since you came down here.'

'Although the relevance of these facts, at this stage, is dubious to say the least.' Holmes added sternly.

By now we had reached the shore and were strolling along a small beach before reaching the main wharves. As we approached Bell Wharf I was amazed at the volume of traffic that so small a town could generate. The principal supply line, for the area, came by way of barges which were unloaded at Bell Wharf. The supplies were then transported to the town centre by a constant stream of carts and boys with barrows. There was even a small tramline which stretched to the heart of Southend.

We negotiated our way through this traffic with some difficulty, then, having passed a bustling boatyard, found ourselves at the base of the coastguard station.

'We shall begin our enquiries here!' Holmes announced.

Fowler and I stared aghast at what Holmes was now proposing. The small wooden office, purporting to be a 'coastguard station', was little more than a shack perched on top of a small pier held over the water's edge by four decaying wooden posts. The staircase, which led to the office door, appeared to be even more precarious, indeed, several missing steps rendered the thing almost impassable and Fowler and I shrugged our shoulders resignedly at the prospect of negotiating them.

To our astonishment Holmes suddenly raced forward and in an instant, was mounting the stairs in just a few hazardous bounds. From the platform he greeted us with a triumphant wave, but, feeling unable to follow him, we could only gaze enviously upward as he disappeared through the office door.

Holmes was not to emerge again from the coastguard's office, for a full hour, and Fowler and I could only speculate idly as to the reason for so long a visit. As was common with someone as enigmatic as Holmes, this would not be made clear to us for some considerable time. During those long sixty minutes Fowler and I marvelled at the endless stream of cocklers who passed by, fully laden on their way to the cockle-sheds, or 'mushers'. The cockles were, indeed, strange looking little creatures, in their natural raw form, but were, evidently, the very life blood of Leigh-on-Sea.

We were whiling away our time by skimming pebbles on the calm estuary waters, when Holmes came bounding down the precarious stairs towards us. He bore the look of a man who had just met with some considerable success.

'Gentlemen, I am glad to see that you have spent your spare hour in so productive a manner!' Holmes laughed.

In a state of some embarrassment, I discreetly sprinkled my remaining pebbles over the ground and then asked: 'I

assume that your time spent in that death trap was somewhat more rewarding?'

'Oh, considerably so. This case has assumed a totally
different aspect as a consequence. However, before I impart
to you of the results of my enquiries, I have been informed
that the views from the summit of Leigh Hill are most gratifying.' Without another word Holmes sprinted up a hill so
steep that someone with a weaker heart would have been
seriously incommoded in its negotiation.

My attempt at restraining him fell on deaf ears and as
usual I was left in his wake and in awe at the boundless
energy he seemed to generate when the scent of success was
upon him. By the time Fowler and I had joined him at the
top of the hill Holmes seemed to have already completed his
surveillance and was resting on a small stone wall, his pipe
well established. He waved this dramatically before him in
a broad sweep.

'It is not often that the entire geographical evidence of a
case is laid before you in just one splendid vista,' Holmes
observed. Fowler and I exchanged puzzled glances.

Having noted this with a little amusement, Holmes
continued, still using his pipe as a pointer. 'To the left we
can see the full width of the estuary, wherein the *Alicia* was
last seen. Below us and to the right, we can make out the
wharf from where she departed, and to the far right are the
mudflats of Two Tree Island, which, as a result of my
enquiries at the coastguard office, have assumed a singular
significance that even I could not have foreseen.'

'For heaven's sake, Holmes!' I exclaimed, by now unable
to contain my frustration at his enigmatic utterances. 'If the
Inspector and I are to take any sort of intelligent interest in
this case you must remember that we were not present with

you at the coastguard's office. If you wish me to return to London, thereby intending to continue your investigation alone, please inform me now and I will return to the hotel and begin my packing immediately!'

'My dear fellow, by no means is it my intention to exclude you, nor do I wish for your premature return to London. Any insight into my nature that you may thus far have gained should assure you that the reticence I might show in expounding upon my theories is born of the specialist's reluctance to show his hand, prior to reaching absolute confidence in their validity. As ever, your continued support and assistance are of the utmost value to me.' As Holmes concluded this lengthy vindication of his behaviour, he placed his hand upon my shoulder to assure me of his sincerity.

Naturally, the playful smile on his lips and the eager intensity in his eyes won me over at once. 'Well, of course I shall stay!' I assured him emphatically.

'Hah, Watson! Well, we have seen enough here, so, Inspector Fowler, if you can suggest somewhere suitable for a decent lunch, I shall outline my itinerary for the coming afternoon, during the course of the meal.'

As it turned out, Fowler's only experience of Leigh's culinary offerings, had been confined to the dining-room of the Peter Boat. Their fish pie was more than above average and even Holmes's normally reluctant appetite was tempted by its delights. We three made short work of our luncheon and a tankard each of local ale and before long, over our pipes, Holmes outlined his immediate plans.

'So as not to incur your wrath still further, friend Watson, I would inform you at once that it is my intention to take the first available train to London, as soon as our meal is concluded.' Holmes now continued hurriedly to prevent my inevitable interjection. 'However, this apparent retreat will only be for the benefit of any interested eyes that may happen to be upon me. I shall alight at Pitsea station and then take the next southbound train to Southend where, I understand, there is a very fine theatre, of whose wardrobe department I shall endeavour to make full use. You see, there is insufficient time for me to return to Baker Street, but it will suit my purposes admirably if certain parties are convinced of my return there.'

'You are so convinced that there is a conspiracy afoot?' I asked quietly.

'We are wading in waters as deep and dark as those of the estuary itself,' Holmes gravely replied. 'Upon my return to Leigh, in my guise as an old sea dog, I fully intend to ingratiate myself with the patrons of the Sailors Rest and find out what I may about Captain Johnson and his unhappy crew.' Having emptied the contents of his pipe into a large glass ashtray, Holmes slowly rose from his chair. 'Should my itinerary go according to plan we shall meet again by the late evening.'

'So I am to remain gainfully unemployed once again?' I asked sarcastically.

'Oh no, it shall be quite the contrary, my dear fellow. It shall fall on you to ensure that word of my departure to London be commonly known. It might be as well to begin with the Lomases themselves. I am sure it will not be long before young Edward informs his employer. Then, I think, an interview with "Uncle Ted" Burnley might be in order. You will, inevitably, gain more insight into a man's true nature from an adversary, than you will ever gain from a close friend or relation.' Then, with a doff of his hat, my old friend was gone.

'Well, Doctor, Mr Holmes certainly seems to know what he is about. I suggest we drop a word or two into the ears of one or two landlords and while you seek out the Lomases I shall search my notes for Mr Burnley's address. Shall we meet back here in, say, one hour? Then we shall see what light Mr Burnley might be able to shed upon this matter.'

I nodded my affirmation enthusiastically, amazed at how willing Fowler was to co-operate with Holmes and his plans.

I felt rather ashamed at having to disturb the Lomases with the fabricated and unwelcome news of Holmes's unscheduled return to London. However, I softened the blow somewhat by assuring them that Holmes had not given up on their father and would be returning to Leigh within the next forty eight hours. Edward accepted the news with apparent indifference, whilst his sister's previous excitable display of disappointment was replaced with a more crestfallen demeanour, for which I felt guilty at having caused.

The news of Holmes's departure was spread further around the community by Fowler and myself informing our respective landlords whilst ensuring that others were within earshot. Satisfied that by nightfall not one resident of Leigh-on-Sea would doubt the certainty of Holmes's departure, Fowler and I kept our appointment to meet at the Peter Boat and immediately set off for the residence of 'Uncle Ted' Burnley.

As it turned out Burnley lived barely a half-mile from the home of his business rival, Nathaniel Garside, in a charming cottage on the New Road. Sadly, the exterior of the cottage and its grounds were in a state of sad neglect, the garden being somewhat overgrown. As we found out, this reflected the chaotic and eccentric nature of its owner.

Burnley's renowned liberal stance on every aspect of social and political life explained the size and nature of his household. A robust, middle-aged lady, called Mary, who answered the summons of our knock on the front door, was the cottage's only other resident and she worked as both housekeeper and cook. However, it was to Burnley's credit, as her employer, that she carried out her many tasks whilst displaying a most cheerful disposition and much enthusiasm.

She showed us into a cluttered drawing room and introduced us to Mr Burnley as he walked towards us from the French windows at the rear of the house. He shook us by the hand with gusto and greeted us with a warm smile, exuding charm from every pore. Without requiring prior instruction, at once Mary promised us a tray of tea, whilst Burnley cleared a couple of armchairs of books before inviting us to be seated with a wave of his arm.

'The poor woman is constantly clearing up after me and, I must confess, it is a mostly perpetual and thankless task. However, in all other aspects I am mostly self-sufficient, so it gives her something to do!' Mary was halfway through the door, on her way for the tea, when Burnley's jibes caught her attention, but she seemed to appreciate his humour without taking offence.

'I must confess that she does not appear to be terribly put upon,' I responded in similar vein. As I was speaking, Burnley busied himself by clearing another heap of books from a chair close to mine and Fowler's, then, perching himself on the edge of his seat he rubbed his hands together as he asked: 'Now gentlemen, you must explain to me how I can be of service to you.'

It felt strange to be taking part in an interview and not being required to take notes. Of course, as a representative of the official force, it was second nature for Fowler to use his notebook and pencil and I, for once, was able to sit back and observe my surroundings and the gentleman we had come to interview.

Edward Burnley was a man of below average height, but of above average girth. Indeed, the ornate gold watch-chain, his pride in which he was locally renowned, seemed likely to snap a link every time he laughed. Although in his mid-sixties, he was blessed with a full head of silver hair, which had been revealed when he removed his colourful checked cap upon entering the room, and this was complemented by a similarly textured beard and moustache. His small brown eyes sparkled from behind the lenses of a pair of steel-rimmed spectacles.

Before Fowler or myself could respond to Burnley's offer of assistance he enlarged upon his question by adding:

'Naturally, I am surprised to receive such a visit, Inspector. I understood that your investigations in Leigh had been concluded and I was equally certain that Mr Holmes's return to London indicated that your own interest in the tragic loss of the *Alicia* was at an end also. Doctor Watson, I am gratified to see, however, that neither of you has been put off by the reputation for ruthlessness which Nathaniel Garside has so justifiably earned.'

'So, you understand the purpose behind our visit, then?' Fowler said quietly.

'Well, Inspector, I felt certain that it would not be a social visit!' Burnley said with his customary red-faced chuckle.

Before we could continue further Mary returned to the room bearing a tray of tea and scones. She stood before Burnley with a frown, indicating the clutter on an occasional table next to him. With mumbled apologies, Burnley hastily removed the offending objects and poured the tea himself after Mary had bustled from the room.

After we had each consumed a scone and taken a sip of tea, Fowler responded to Burnley in a manner that certainly surprised me.

'To be candid then, sir, at the outset of my investigation I had been hampered in performing my duty by both Garside's reputation and his undoubted influence both on the local community and my own superiors.

'However, certain arguments put forward by Mr Holmes have convinced me that there may be more than an element of truth in old man Lomas's original statement, despite its apparently implausible assertions. In fact, I can now readily admit that my desire to further my own career, by pleasing my superiors, has led to an innocent man's incarceration, the suffering of his family and the destroying of his reputation. I am certain that, but for Mr Holmes's intervention, these wrongs would not have been righted.' In a state of red-faced embarrassment Fowler paused for a moment.

'You do realize, Inspector, that in accepting Lomas's version of events you are acknowledging the probability that the *Alicia* had been deliberately scuppered?' Burnley asked.

'I do,' Fowler replied emphatically.

'Equally, I am sure you are aware that the likely culprit would prove to be none other than the *Alicia*'s owner, Nathaniel Garside. Therefore you have come to me, his well-known business rival, in the hope that I might provide you with a credible motive.' There was no hint of admonishment in Burnley's voice, indeed, he seemed to be full of admiration for Fowler's honesty.

'You have a full and accurate grasp of the situation, Mr Burnley,' Fowler replied, raising his eyes to him in hopeful expectantly.

'Well then, you should be glad to hear that I might just be able to provide you with the information that you require.' The sparkle returned to Burnley's eyes and he helped himself to some more of his tea.

At Burnley's words I was at once filled with the thrill of anticipation, although I am ashamed to admit that it was more at the thought of Holmes's reaction to my supplying vital information for once, rather than the actual prospect of Burnley's imminent statement.

'Despite my well-publicized misgivings regarding the ethics behind the majority of Garside's business dealings, the local community still regard him with misguided trust and respect. However, one could equally put this down to fear, when you bear in mind how many people within the community depend upon him for their livelihood. His business interests range from numerous shops, boatyards, "mushers", or cockle-sheds, to a controlling interest in the gas company. In this last capacity, and to his credit, he was instrumental in the laying on of gas and public street-lighting, and he has undoubtedly improved the local highways during his chairmanship of the parish council.

'Unfortunately, none of this seems to be enough for him. His employees are grotesquely underpaid and maltreated and, because he just happens to be their landlord, they are forced to live in horrendously sordid conditions, paying nearly all of their paltry wages for the privilege!'

'It does not seem to me that a man in his eminent position should need to bother himself with the disposal of an antique and redundant vessel,' I conjectured. 'Much less the fate of a rum-sodden old seaman.'

'I agree with you sir!' Burnley responded. 'Yet I have, subsequently, discovered that Lloyd's are liable to pay considerable compensation for the *Alicia*'s untimely loss, and before you ask me why a man of his wealth should go to such lengths and take such risks merely to realize an old insurance policy, I shall tell you.

'Nathaniel Garside is not, as he would like to be regarded, an honourable man. He is a pathological gambler! Gentlemen, do not be deceived by the fact that I appear more liberal and freethinking than my rival, for I am none the less a businessman and possess all the acumen and wiliness of one in my profession. Consequently, I have been able to ascertain, through various business acquaintances, that Garside is not in the sound financial position that one would assume.

'Gentlemen, I am sure you will agree that the motive of Garside shoring up his crumbling empire with the proceeds from the insurance company, would be a strong one?'

Fowler and I agreed most emphatically, but then declined Burnley's offer of further hospitality, wishing to be present at the hotel when Holmes made his return As it turned out we were back at the Ship hotel well before Holmes arrived, and our vigil in the bar was a long, albeit, comfortable one.

By the time Holmes did stride into the saloon all the other guests had long retired to their rooms and the barkeeper was impatiently waiting for Fowler and myself to drain the dregs of our pints and knock out our final pipes.

'So good of you to wait up for me! I must apologize for the lateness of the hour. Bartender! I think a round of Cognacs is in order. Oh, and one for yourself, of course,' Holmes added, at his most charmingly persuasive, clearly observant of the man's annoyance at the lateness of the hour. However, we received our Cognacs and retired with them to the comfortable armchairs.

Holmes's appearance was most peculiar. His face was flushed with success and yet was undoubtedly exhausted from his efforts. Remnants of his impersonation of an old sea dog still clung to his hair and cheeks and he plucked at these impatiently while we sat there talking.

'So, Watson, your countenance smacks of self-satisfaction. I assume, therefore, that you have important information to impart,' Holmes speculated.

'That honour should fall to my colleague from Scotland Yard,' I replied gesturing towards the inspector.

Then to the dismay of both Fowler and myself, and just as Fowler was about to bring out his notebook, Holmes launched into a narrative of his own, before either of us was able to utter a single word. However, and to his credit, Holmes noticed our crestfallen faces. He broke off in mid-sentence, and gestured towards Fowler and his book. 'Perhaps your information will render mine redundant,' he suggested.

It became clear, however, that his statement was not born of humility, for this was not a virtue with which Holmes was particularly well-endowed; it sprang more from the certain knowledge that this would not prove to be the case. However, he listened patiently and in silence whilst Fowler read from his notes.

'Ah, gentlemen, if only you had acted upon your information at once, rather than rushing back here to impart it to me! Alas this remissness of yours, has now led to our bird having flown his coop!' Holmes immediately countered this admonishment by adding: 'Do not be dismayed, though, for an astute station clerk observed Garside boarding a train bound for Fenchurch Street and, even now, Inspector Fowler, your colleagues, should be meeting his train on its arrival. However, his far more malevolent colleague is still at large here in Leigh and I expect his arrival in but a few minutes.' This last sentence Holmes uttered in a whisper.

'I do not understand,' I said. 'Surely Captain Johnson was with you earlier. Why should you require him to present himself here, now, at this ungodly hour?'

'Oh Watson, you still do not understand the precept that I have long preached of the dangers of forming false assumptions. Captain Johnson, to whom I have promised an unhindered retreat from Leigh, by the way, was only Garside's confederate in the attempt to defraud the insurers. The true and far more sinister motive for the sinking of the *Alicia* was known to only one other and it is that individual's arrival that I am now expecting here shortly.' As he spoke, Holmes finally achieved success in removing the last piece of false whisker from the side of his face. With a sigh of grateful relief he lit a cigarette and sat back in his chair so that he could study our expressions with an air of amused anticipation.

'I am not certain that you have the authority to grant such immunity.' Fowler sternly commented, echoing my own thoughts, although I had been witness on many occasions to Holmes dispensing his own brand of justice.

'Very likely not, Inspector, however, I am sure that once I set before you the true nature of the crime, and the part that Captain Johnson has played in bringing about the apprehension of the worst of its perpetrators, you will not judge me too harshly!'

Suddenly, Holmes leant forward, pressing his bony elbows down into his equally bony knees. 'Perhaps,' he went on mischievously, 'it would be best if I fill in the missing pieces of this most tortuous puzzle, once our eminent caller has said his piece.' However, upon observing the look of indignation upon our faces, he partly relented.

'Very well then, although I am inhibited by lack of time from providing you with a full discourse, let me then lay before you certain significant points that you have not, so far, been privy to, but which should allow you to reach the same conclusion as I have arrived at. Despite their apparent lack of relevance, I entreat you both to refrain from comment until you have been able to digest them all.'

Fowler took advantage of the brief pause while Holmes lit up his pipe, to sharpen his pencil and light a cigarette of his own.

'You are aware, of course that Nathaniel Garside is responsible for the upkeep and maintenance of the local highways, but not, perhaps of the fact that many of his labourers are drafted in from the ranks of prisoners sentenced to hard labour. I learnt from my friends in the coastguard office that a man as callous as Garside thought nothing of removing these men from their highway duties and drafting them in to his small army of cocklers. His attitude towards their safety was nothing less than cavalier and on the afternoon prior to the *Alicia*'s final voyage, the coastguards observed Garside collect the men from the creek, long after the tide had begun its slow journey towards land. When you bear in mind the fact that the mudflats of Two Tree Island are notoriously liable to sudden flooding and that these unfortunate men are required to remove the cockles by rake from the sand right up to the moment before Garside arrives with his boat and nets, you can well understand the coastguards' concern for the men's safety. However they took no action because when Garside eventually returned to shore, all appeared to be well with the men on board his boat. They thought no more of it, because they had not noticed a small report in the local news sheet that told of two members of the highway work party escaping from their guards, on the very day in question.'

Holmes was clearly warming to his theme and all thoughts of his mysterious guest's arrival seemed to have been dispelled for the moment. He paused to light his pipe once more, staring strangely at Fowler and myself as he did so. 'Ha! so the light of realization is at last illuminating your grasp of matters, I observe!' Holmes suddenly exclaimed.

Fowler and I exchanged glances, then nodded our affirmation emphatically. For my own part, the disjointed facts that Holmes had just volleyed towards us had built up a picture of a most dreadful and inhumane crime. But I was still at a loss as to the identity of our eagerly awaited visitor.

'I am certain, therefore, that when I tell you that Captain Johnson confirmed to me that he had personally scuppered the *Alicia* to help his employer ease his financial difficulties by way of the coffers of his insurers, you will not be particularly surprised. More interestingly, however, was his assertion that the hold of the vessel, which he personally inspects thoroughly before any voyage, contained two large barrels that had not been present the night before. These Garside must have loaded in the dead of night and, because of their size and weight, with the help of one other—'

'Holmes,' I interrupted, 'you are so certain that this "other" could not have been Captain Johnson, that you allowed him freedom to go on his way?'

'Watson, he would hardly have mentioned the barrels at all were he not innocent of the act. I would have had no other means of knowing of their existence, seeing that they now rest on the bottom of the Channel.'

'No, no, of course not,' I hurriedly and abashedly admitted. 'Then who else would have aided Garside in his awful deception? Another member of the crew?'

'I think not; they were unreservedly loyal to Johnson, to the last man. No, the person we are looking for is someone as ruthlessly ambitious as his master and one who would stop at nothing to preserve his job and career—'

'Even if it meant seeing his own father unjustly incarcerated to further his ambition?' Another voice callously asked this question from the entrance to the saloon. After all I had just heard and understood; even I was not surprised to see the sneering figure of Edward Lomas standing there.

'I apologize for the lateness of my arrival, but from the moment that I received your note, I knew that the game was up. If the all-powerful Nathaniel Garside had found it impossible to escape from you, Mr Holmes, what chance, then had I, his underling? Besides I have heard enough from behind the door to know that any defence or resistance now would be futile.' Despite these words of bravado, beads of perspiration on his brow and a tremor in his right hand indicated that Lomas was surely affected by the situation. As though to confirm this he made for the bar and drank hungrily from a large glass of cognac.

Then he sank wearily into an armchair opposite ours and acknowledged the presence of both Fowler and myself with the briefest of nods. Upon hearing the metallic sound of Fowler rummaging in his pockets for a set of handcuffs, Lomas said, 'I can assure you, Inspector, that there will be no need for those. If nothing else, I am a man who knows when he has been bettered.'

Fowler, however, ignored his words and applied the cuffs with a rapid certainty.

'Very well, Inspector, but before you drag me off to your cell, I beseech you all not to judge me too harshly,' Lomas said, his tone of voice mellowing somewhat.

'Really sir!' I reproached him. 'It is hard not to do so!'

'Perhaps, but consider; it is not easy for an ambitious young man to make a life for himself in a village like Leigh-on-Sea. With a young sister to support and a father with a pronounced leaning to drink, it was not easy to stay out of the clutches of a man such as Nathaniel Garside. Besides the men in the barrels were only convicted prisoners,' Lomas concluded.

'Perhaps they were,' Holmes rejoined. 'Yet they were still entitled to a better fate than falling victim to avariciousness and greed. It hurts me to know that despite all my efforts at bringing the full weight of British justice down upon you, your fate should prove to be less unhappy than theirs!' Acting upon an indication from Holmes, Fowler began to remove his chained prisoner from the room, only to be confronted by the tearful Miss Lomas leaning on the doorframe.

'Oh, Edward!' she screamed. 'How could you, your own father?'

Before Lomas could reply, Fowler finished hauling him out of the room and I raced to the girl's side to guide her over to a chair, for she could now hardly stand.

Then, to my great surprise, Holmes crouched down before her and took her by the hand.

'My dear young lady, I assure you that I take no satisfaction from the conclusion of this case. My great regret is that on the very night that I have been able to restore your father to you, I have been compelled to remove your brother.' As the girl's tears began to fall on Holmes's hand, he became momentarily embarrassed and, inevitably, it was left for me to comfort her.

An interesting postscript to the events just described was our discovery of the fate of Captain Johnson's crew. Apparently they had been sufficiently rewarded by Garside to have been able to buy a small fishing vessel of their own, which they operate successfully out of Grimsby. Their escape from the *Alicia* was achieved by virtue of a small dinghy, attached to the larger craft. Its towline had been severed by a knife ... with a serrated edge!

THE ADVENTURE OF THE RED LEECH

*'... I see my notes upon the repulsive story of the red leech
and the terrible death of Crosby, the banker ...'*
(*The Adventure of Golden Pince-Nez* by A. Conan Doyle)

'Well, well, friend Watson, I perceive that a matrimonial fracas, at "Castle Watson" has brought you to my door this morning.' Holmes mischievously observed one bright spring morning, during the years of my marriage to my beloved Mary.

As a result of my long association with Sherlock Holmes I had been witness to many examples of my friend's extraordinary powers and yet he had still not lost the ability to surprise me. I had just taken to my old familiar chair by the fireside and was slowly unfolding my unread morning paper as Holmes greeted me with this amazing statement. My paper fell from my grasp, for I knew from past experience that this was neither guesswork nor conjecture on his part.

My mood and disposition were such that on this occasion I had no great desire to express my amazement. 'Evidently I have not been altogether successful at concealing my frame of mind this morning!' I snapped whilst reclaiming my paper from the floor.

'On the contrary, my dear fellow, I merely reached my conclusion from the fact that the redoubtable Mrs Watson would not, under normal circumstances, allow you to leave the house wearing unpolished shoes and both a brown and black stocking,' Holmes remarked with some amusement.

I glanced down to confirm that I was, indeed, wearing a different colour on each foot.

Ignoring my embarrassment, Holmes continued: 'On the only other occasion that I have observed such a sartorial calamity, Mrs Watson had taken herself away for a few weeks to visit her people. I recall your lamenting such a visit barely a month ago, so she is patently not due for another for some time to come. Therefore there must be another reason for her apathy towards your appearance this morning. Your early arrival and your undoubtedly grouchy demeanour merely confirm my simple deduction!' With a dramatic, self-congratulatory wave of his arms Holmes sank back into his chair once more.

'Merely a trifle,' I responded quietly. 'Just a trifle. However I observe that there may be a means for you to put your powers to more productive use and an explanation for your own light mood.' I remarked whilst pointing towards a small piece of paper on the arm of Holmes's chair.

'Well then, pour your nervous energy into providing me with your conclusions regarding this!' Holmes leapt up from his chair and tossed the note into my lap on his way to the mantelpiece, where he filled his pipe from the Persian slipper.

My newspaper now forgotten, I hurriedly unfolded what was, potentially, the road to a new adventure.

'Why, there is nothing here at all!' I exclaimed with much disappointment.

The note was a simple one:

I would appreciate a consultation, any
time after sunset on the 14th.
Yours, RANDELL CROSBY.

'Watson! After all that you have observed and chronicled of my methods over the years you seem to have learnt nothing. Do not merely read the words of the note. Deduce!'

Somewhat put out, I filled a pipe of my own, while formulating my observations. 'Evidently the matter is of some importance, for today is surely the 14th, besides which, the brief, untidy nature of the writing seems also to indicate urgency. It is almost as if the note was written off the cuff because the paper used has surely been torn from a larger sheet and the tool used was a most blunt pencil. Other than these points, I can deduce nothing.'

Holmes clapped his hands together gleefully. 'Excellent Watson! Evidently your domestic dramas have sharpened your faculties. However, valid as your observations undoubtedly are, your conclusions are somewhat wide of the mark. For example, if Mr Crosby's situation was as dire as you presume it to be why does he request an evening consultation? I would have been more persuaded of its urgency had he arrived here before you! Furthermore, I am convinced that the ragged state of his writing materials is due more to his impoverished position than to any lack of thought. See here the black thumbmark on the bottom right-hand corner. Of course none of this means that there is no urgency involved, but there are certainly other factors to be taken into consideration.'

I nodded gravely. 'Why should he be so insistent on arriving after sunset? It is a most unusual turn of phrase.'

'For the answer to that we shall have to await the evening,' Holmes replied.

'We?' I queried his assumption.

'I had hoped that you would be prepared to spend the day in my company. I am certain that Mrs Hudson is well able to double the rations of supper, and perhaps you might aid me in my interview of the nocturnal Randell Crosby. Unless, of course, you have some more pressing matters elsewhere?'

'Not at all.' I smiled. 'I should be delighted!'

'Ha! That is more like the Watson of old.' Holmes laughed.

As it turned out, Mrs Hudson was well able to accommodate me for both luncheon and supper and to my great surprise Holmes was only too willing to help me collate the notes of our most recently completed case. Normally he took little interest in my 'humble scratchings', however the *Adventure of the Aspiring Architect* had proved to be such a personal triumph for Holmes and his seldom reported ability of transposing himself into the place of the criminal by way of meditation, that he wished to ensure that the story was laid out correctly.

Although I was subsequently duty bound to embellish the story with sufficient dramatic content to satisfy my public, by the time the supper things had been removed and the sun had gone down, we were both reasonably satisfied with the results of our labour. It had soon become quite dark outside and we now prepared ourselves for the visit of Randell Crosby.

Alas, even upon our first glance at the poor fellow, Holmes's assessment of Crosby's impecunious circumstances was confirmed. Holmes, of course, thought nothing of such things, but I was certain that Mrs Hudson, had she been present, would have taken pains to cover her chair before allowing Crosby access to it.

Crosby shuffled slowly into the room, his gait that of a man twenty years his senior, although, as we learned later he was only thirty-five years of age. He was of average height, although his stoop rendered him shorter. He wore an old greatcoat, two sizes too large for him and caked in grime, a dusty bowler, and a long scarf that covered most of his pale unshaven face. When he spoke it was in a surprisingly modulated tone, albeit at a volume so soft that he was barely audible.

'I must apologize both for my appearance and the lateness of the hour, gentlemen, and yet I am certain that once I have explained my situation you will surely bear me forgiveness.'

Holmes smiled sympathetically towards him and waved him towards a spare seat.

'Mr Crosby, please explain to me in precise detail the true nature of your predicament and how you consider that I might be of assistance to you,' Holmes requested quietly.

Clearly uncomfortable in these surroundings and incommoded by his personal circumstances and attire, Crosby repeatedly shifted nervously on the edge of his seat.

'Calm yourself, Mr Crosby,' Holmes kindly reassured him. 'Perhaps a glass of Cognac and a Dutch panatella might go some way towards easing your nerves,' he suggested, indicating to me that I should supply these aids.

Crosby gratefully received both the drink and cigar. He bowed his head. 'Both very fine indeed, gentlemen.'

'Mr Crosby, you have evidently been both raised and educated as a gentleman. Perhaps you might find it easier to begin by explaining how you have come to your present circumstance.' Holmes proposed.

'That will prove to be easier than you might think. Whilst it is true that my upbringing was very much as you have suggested, it was also obvious, from a very early age, that it would not always be so.' Crosby drew upon his cigar and sipped from his glass before continuing.

'In order that you might not preconceive any judgement upon my family, I should immediately point out that they had experienced much anguish and no little expense in determining both my condition and how best to cope with its consequences.'

Observing my own quizzical glance at the mention of the word 'condition' Crosby directed his next words in my direction. 'Even allowing for your vast knowledge and experience, Dr Watson, I am certain that not even you will have heard of "Solar Urticaria".'

'Upon my word, I have not!' I exclaimed, whilst making my way towards the small remnant of my medical library that still remained in Baker Street.

Crosby called me to a halt. 'Do not trouble yourself, Doctor, for I can assure you that my own experience has given me a knowledge of the condition that will far exceed anything that your learned volume might provide. As its very name suggests, "Solar Utricaria" is aggravated by exposure to direct sunlight. Even bright daylight might produce an effect on the skin.'

Having sensed Crosby's hesitation Holmes prompted: 'And what effect is this, Mr Crosby?'

'Monstrous large red welts, the size of leeches, immediately form on every unprotected surface of my skin the very instant that it is exposed to natural light. The effect that this apparition had on any observer soon made it obvious to my parents that it would be impossible for me to leave the confines of our home during the hours of daylight.'

'Good Lord, how awful!' I exclaimed. 'Of course, that would explain your unusually pale complexion.'

'Indeed.' Crosby gravely acknowledged my comment with a slow nodding of his head, 'Due to the fact that these welts are slow to disappear, socializing, of every description was impossible. I was even educated at home! My beloved parents employed the very best private tutors who taught me well in every subject. However as I grew older I came to realize that the strain of the burden upon my parents, both emotionally and financially, was proving too great to bear. This despite the fact that they took great pains to conceal it.' Crosby then paused for a moment to draw gratefully upon his cigar and to sip at his brandy.

'Their love and compassion knew no bounds. So I then resolved to spare them further heartbreak by taking my leave of the family home. My brother, Nathaniel, was proving a great success at his chosen career of banking and I was certain that he would prove to be a great comfort to them as they mourned my departure.

'Therefore, at the age of thirty-two, with but a few posses-sions and a little allowance money that I had managed to save, I found myself in an outside world of which I had very little knowledge and experience. In order to avoid the atten-tions of those whom my parents might set to finding me, I resolved to travel. I managed to ingratiate myself with the owners of a small travelling carnival that was, fortuitously, heading towards the West Country. I kept my head covered during the day and worked with the keeper at feeding and cleaning out the various creatures that formed part of the show. The owners, Mr and Mrs Josiah Smythe of Blackheath, were most kind to me and gave me board and a small allowance for my efforts. However there were two caravan drivers, with a leaning towards drink, whose curiosity as to my covered head was becoming increasingly difficult to ward off.

'I had two friends among the workers with the carnival. A young lad called Tom, who had an unusually small head; he was one of the sideshow attractions under the moniker of "Pin Head". The other was the animal keeper, "Old Ben", an elderly fellow, from the East End of London who was half-blind. These two tried to shelter me from the attentions of the two unsavouries. However, I found myself alone one morning with the horses, and during the course of a violent scuffle with the drivers I found my head covering removed and my awful secret was exposed.

'The drivers took great pains to reveal my appearance to all in the camp and I was resolved upon making a hasty departure, when the Smythes made me an unusual proposal.

'Business had become quite slack of late, so they suggested that I should share his enclosure with Tom and appear as the "Red Leech". In this way I should become one of the sideshow attractions. The idea of becoming a fairground freak appalled me at first, as you might well imagine.'

He paused for a moment, scanning our faces for signs of understanding and, perhaps, a little sympathy. I looked across at Holmes and was amazed to observe how intently my friend was gazing into the eyes of our tragic client. The man's obvious pain was mirrored in the eyes of the habitually ice-cold Sherlock Holmes.

Then, as if remembering himself, he suddenly straightened up and remarked: 'Although your story has a certain poignancy about it I would now appreciate it if you could proceed to the crux of the matter, Mr Crosby. You might begin by explaining why you agreed to become the "Red Leech".'

Understandably taken aback by Holmes's biting outburst, Crosby apologetically cleared his throat and stumbled over his first few words.

'I could see that Tom had never been maltreated or humiliated; indeed he even regarded the carnival as a form of refuge from the somewhat harsher treatment he might have expected from the world outside. Therefore I resolved to accept the offer that I had received from the Smythes. The arrangement suited both parties; for a time. I was content with my modest accommodation and keep and the "Red Leech" was proving to be a popular and profitable attraction for the Smythes, which pleased me also. It all ended somewhat abruptly, however, when I chanced upon a week-old copy of the *Times*.

'Therein, gentlemen, almost hidden in a column listing recent deaths was the first intimation that I had received of my parent's untimely passing. They had always been keen explorers and, as a consequence, were aboard a small steam transport, which had been wrecked but a few miles off the East African coast. No trace of them or their belongings were ever recovered.

'I decided to return to London at once, there to seek out my brother for more information than the newspaper afforded and to discuss any family arrangements that might concern me. Ben, the old animal keeper, kindly accompanied me, as he knew of a small basement room in a run-down old building near Brick Lane. He offered to run any urgent errands that could only be accomplished in daylight. I had no great difficulty in finding my brother, as he had yet to vacate the family home, and I found his welcome somewhat warmer than I might have expected. However, he reluctantly informed me at the outset, that my parents had been so convinced either of my death or my inability ever to return to them, that no provision had been made for me in their final will.

'To his credit, Nathaniel was not insensitive to my reaction to this news, nor could he have failed to observe the very obvious physical effects of my present situation. There and then he resolved to make me a small monthly allowance. He explained that his imminent wedding was proving to be a most costly affair and that our parents' estate had proved in the end to be a surprisingly modest one, probably eaten away by the costs of their insatiable lust for travel. The amount was barely sufficient to keep body and soul together, but I was grateful even for that.

'I did not wish to embarrass my brother by revealing my address to him, so it was agreed that he would deposit the money at a large newsagent's on the Commercial Road on the first Monday of every month. My friend Ben collected it regularly and this meagre sum was supplemented by my night cleaning job and any small errands that Ben was able to run for the local traders. By these means we were somehow able to survive.

'You may therefore understand my consternation when upon one Monday, now two months ago, Ben returned from our friend the newsagent empty-handed. I have implicit trust in old Ben and he, in turn, trusts the newsagent, so I had to assume that my brother had withheld the money for his own reasons. I decided to visit my family home once more, in the hope that the missing money was nothing more than an oversight. I was distraught to discover that the place had been boarded up and was on offer for sale, whilst the only information that I could glean from the neighbours was that my brother had been married and had moved away.

'For reasons that I have now explained to you, I am not able to conduct any enquiries into Nathaniel's whereabouts on my own account and the police would be aghast at the thought of granting me an interview. Although, I am sure, you will have far loftier matters that demand your attention, I turn to you, Mr Holmes, as the only recourse I have of restoring what scant means of subsistence remains to me.' Crosby drained the last of his brandy and extinguished his cigar as he concluded his moving and remarkable story.

For a moment Holmes sat silent and still. He then jumped up and strode to the window, through which he gazed wistfully, strumming his bony fingers against its glass.

Holmes's voice was barely audible when he next spoke.

'You must understand, Mr Crosby, that this is not the kind of routine inquiry with which I normally involve myself. However,' he added quickly so as not to lower Crosby's spirits still further, 'I am curious to discover the true reason behind the withholding of the money and you have surely suffered much already. If you give the address of your newsagent to Dr Watson here, I promise to leave word of your brother's whereabouts there within a week.' With a dismissive wave of the hand, Holmes turned his gaze towards Baker Street once more.

As he slowly rose to take his leave Crosby added: 'Your reputation for cleverness has been well documented by Dr Watson, but your kindness and compassion should be lauded equally.' Holmes responded with only the briefest of nods, but maintained his vigil by the window until Crosby had shuffled out of sight towards the Marylebone Road.

For a moment after Crosby had disappeared from view Holmes and I remained both silent and still, Holmes continuing to linger by the window and myself leaning against the door that I had just closed behind our long-suffering client.

'So, Watson, what are we to make of all this, then?' Holmes asked, turning away from the window and lighting a cigarette.

'Well, I suppose the story itself is a simple enough one and its conclusion is that the size of the parents' estate precluded the newly married, Nathaniel Crosby from continuing to live in the family home. I presume that he has now moved to a somewhat less salubrious area and has decided that his brother's meagre allowance was an expense that he could ill afford.'

Holmes eyed me quizzically for a moment and then grunted absent-mindedly as he extinguished his cigarette in a half-empty coffee cup.

'Yours does seem to be the likeliest of explanations, yet such action would appear to be out of character. Remember how Randell described the warmth of the greeting that he received from his brother? Besides which, he was not coerced into granting his brother an allowance; it was his own idea, no matter how inadequate it proved to be. No, I am convinced that there is another reason for the money's being withheld,' Holmes quietly concluded.

'Perhaps some form of ill-fortune has overtaken him,' I suggested whilst gathering my things together.

Holmes barely acknowledged me as I bade him a goodnight. 'Perhaps I shall see you once my enquiries into this matter have gathered pace?' he called, as I was halfway down the stairs.

I spent the following morning making my peace with Mary and then found, over the next few days, that my practice was being overburdened by the victims of a quite virulent strain of influenza. This minor outbreak lasted but a short while, however, and my thoughts returned once more to the plight of Randell Crosby. It was not that my heart had been indifferent to his cause, rather that I had absolute confidence in Holmes's ability to find Nathaniel without any great difficulty.

I was proved correct in making this assumption, to the extent that Holmes was already deeply immersed in his subsequent problem by the time I next visited my old rooms. I found Holmes hunched over a glass jar, in the centre of the dining-table, studying its contents with such an intensity that he scarcely acknowledged my entrance. According to Mrs Hudson, who showed some concern, he had been thus engaged for a number of hours.

'A junior scientist such as yourself might find the contents of this jar of some passing interest,' he uttered mischievously as I quietly approached the table.

Vainly trying to stifle my indignation, I exclaimed: 'Well, I am certainly enough of a scientist to recognize that this is nothing more remarkable than a worm!'

'Watson, you must not allow yourself to be so affected by my little jibes. If you can control your nerves for a moment and observe our small friend with a little more attention you will come to realize that this is, indeed, a most remarkable worm and one completely unknown to science!'

'How did you come to be in possession of so remarkable a creature?' I asked mockingly. 'Does it form the basis of your latest case?'

Indignantly, Holmes hastily covered the jar with a napkin and led me towards our chairs and the Persian slipper. 'This is a matter that can wait for another time, for I am certain that you wish to know the outcome of the Randell Crosby affair.'

'Well of course I do ... but that worm—'

Holmes stopped me in my tracks. 'Desist!' Obediently I sat down and lit my pipe.

'As you might well imagine, the searching out of Nathaniel Crosby was a routine matter that presented me with no great difficulties. Posing as a potential buyer of Crosby's vacant house, I was soon able to extract his present address from the agent handling the sale. Then, masquerading as a cockney hawker, I was able to fall into conversation with a senior member of Crosby's household. From this loquacious individual I discovered that Crosby was now in the employ of Kyle and Onstott's, a small yet most influential bank in Cheapside, where Crosby is expected to do very well.

'Of more interest to me, however, was this individual's opinion of the lady of the house.' Holmes paused for a moment to relight his old clay pipe.

'Really, Holmes!' I interrupted. 'It is not like you to have any truck with idle household gossip.'

'Have I not told you, Watson, on more than one occasion, that a trained student of human nature can glean more relevant information over a pint of ale with the clientele at a saloon bar, than he can from a thousand police reports!' Holmes retorted, hurling his still lighted match to the floor with a flourish as he spoke.

I mumbled apologetically as I fell to the floor to douse the offending flame.

Having composed himself with a long draw upon his pipe, Holmes resumed.

'Upon learning that the woman was both vain and cold-hearted in her meanness, I decided that a visit to the newsagent on the Commercial Road might be in order if I was to present a complete picture of the situation to brother Randell. My suspicions were soon borne out as the newsagent recognized at once my description of the banker's wife of ill-repute. It was she who demanded that the money should now be passed to her and not to old Ben. He was to inform Ben that the money had simply not arrived and to make no mention of her visit.'

'How do you suppose that she discovered her husband's little deception?' I asked, as Holmes paused to re-light his pipe.

'The servant, whose evidence you valued so contemptuously, thinks that she observed her husband handing the footman an envelope, in a most strange and cautious manner. Interestingly enough this individual was dismissed but a few days ago. I have informed Crosby of this in a brief note and I now fully expect him to arrange a clandestine meeting with his brother. As to its results, I am sure Crosby will inform us of them at some future date,' Holmes concluded quietly.

Any further thoughts that we might have had on the subject were suddenly dispelled by a disturbance in the passageway below. Even before we could take steps to investigate its cause, an awkward-looking, red-faced young constable burst into our rooms, with an apologetic Mrs Hudson in close attendance.

'I am so sorry, Mr Holmes ...' she began, before Holmes dismissed her with a wave of his hand.

'Now, Constable,' Holmes spoke quietly and with a smile, 'calm yourself for a moment and then explain the reason behind your clumsy intrusion.'

'Yes sir. Sorry sir. You see, Inspector Lestrade was most insistent that you come at once. I have never seen him so put out before,' the lad replied.

'Where are we to come and with what purpose?' I asked.

'To the Kyle and Onstott bank, of Cheapside, although the inspector would rather inform you himself of the reason for the visit once you have arrived. I have a hansom waiting outside,' he added hopefully.

Holmes gestured for me not to express my astonishment at the mention of the name of the bank.

'We shall join you outside shortly,' Holmes informed the relieved young policeman. Then quietly to me he added: 'We shall learn a lot more from Lestrade for so long as he remains ignorant of our earlier involvement in this matter.' I nodded my agreement and a moment later we were racing down the stairs to the waiting cab.

We were fortunate in that the driver was none other than an old acquaintance of Holmes. George had assisted Holmes in his enquiries on more than one occasion, most notably during the affair of the Naval Treaty, and his intimate knowledge of London enabled us to answer Lestrade's request for urgency most promptly.

We made our way through a veritable labyrinth of security systems before we reached the small but very deep main vault. I have seen Lestrade, many times at the scene of a dreadful crime, but never before have I seen his small weaselly face so etched with distress and confusion. Nor have I seen him so pleased upon Holmes's arrival at the scene.

'Good of you to come, Mr Holmes. This really is something right up your alley,' Lestrade said slowly, trying to calm himself.

Holmes paid scant regard to this dubious greeting and was immediately engaged in his initial survey of the room, whilst gesturing to me to examine the bloodied, lifeless form that lay prostrate in the centre of the vault floor. My examination was as brief as it was futile. The police surgeon would be able to supply a far more detailed report than I was capable of providing in these circumstances. However I was able to confirm that the poor fellow had suffered an almighty blow, to the back of the head, and that a large blunt object, evidently removed at the time of the murder, had been the tool of the man's destruction.

As I gradually stood away from the body I became aware of Holmes slithering across the floor, as if he were a black mamba stalking its prey, with a small magnifying glass protruding from the stalk-like fingers of his left hand. From time to time he would emit a grunt of disappointment. Then he might put a certain object which was invisible to the rest of us under closer examination by raising it to his eye. At last he sprang up from the floor and dusted himself down with a flourish.

'Any clues?' Lestrade asked, a note of hope in his voice, quite unlike his usual cynicism.

'Only three of any real relevance, although I am certain that there would have been considerably more had you and your men not stampeded all over them!' Holmes glared towards two embarrassed constables who were standing to attention by the door, as he spat out these words.

'Three?' Lestrade asked, smiling tentatively.

'However I shall not be able to determine their true

worth until you furnish me with a few facts! For example, have you managed to establish the identity of the victim?'

'Certainly, it is none other than the bank's manager himself, one Nathaniel Crosby.' As Lestrade said this name Holmes shot me a barely discernible glance in the hope that it might prevent me from registering any form of recognition. In this Homes was successful, for Lestrade continued, unaware of our interchange.

'The facts, as I understand them, are as meagre as they are unusual. Crosby informed his staff that he would be working late this very evening in preparation for the regular quarterly audit. At a quarter past seven his chief clerk, John Clevedon, asked if he could be of any further assistance. Crosby informed him that the remainder of his work would need to be conducted in the vault and was for his eyes alone.

'You can, therefore, understand Clevedon's surprise when, upon leaving for the night, he was certain that he heard two agitated voices echoing up from the vault and that one of them was surely that of a woman!'

'A woman?' I questioned. 'Well, perhaps it was that of his wife?'

'That was Clevedon's notion, however he felt that it would be indiscreet of him to try to confirm this, and he continued on his way out of the building. It was at this point, as he turned the last key in the main door to the street, that he heard a most terrible cry that also emanated from the vault. His first instinct was to retrace his steps and to discover the cause of this ghastly sound. However, and to his regret, he thought it unwise to return unattended and so he went in search of a constable—'

Holmes slapped his forehead in exasperation. 'I presume that the search took longer than he had anticipated and that by the time he had returned, policeman in tow, the culprit had long since departed?'

'You have it in one, Mr Holmes,' Lestrade confirmed gravely.

'I presume that your early suspicions have fallen on Crosby's wife?' I asked.

Lestrade nodded emphatically. 'Indeed, Doctor, and I immediately dispatched two men to the Crosby's address. However no one in their small household had a notion as to her whereabouts, so I left an officer there to await her return. So far I have received no word of her.'

'Was the bank fully secured when Clevedon eventually returned?' Holmes asked quietly.

'It was necessary for Clevedon to unlock each lock in the sequence,' Lestrade confirmed.

'Sequence?' Holmes repeated quietly and enigmatically. As he did so he raised himself on to a large chest that stood in a corner of the room. Once there he sat down, cross-legged and with his eyes tightly shut. Lestrade glanced quizzically at him and I turned him away to ask further questions of him.

'What is this sequence you speak of?'

'The main locking device has been arranged in such a way that the final bolt can only be activated provided that the others have been thrown in a particular order. Interestingly, only Clevedon and Crosby were in possession of this sequence and they have both committed it to memory.'

'Well then!' I exclaimed. 'Surely this confirms Mrs Crosby as the murderess. She must have observed her husband lock the door on a previous visit to the bank, and retained memory of the sequence!'

Lestrade shook his head slowly and despondently. 'Ah,

but there is the mystery, Doctor. Clevedon knows of no such visit, the device cannot be fathomed merely by chance and there was not time for her to try every permutation.'

As Lestrade said these words I glanced once again at the forgotten form in the centre of the room. 'This man has only been dead for a little under an hour!' I declared. 'Yet his pallor is that of a far older corpse.'

At this, Holmes's grey, glistening eyes burst suddenly open. He unravelled himself and dropped to the floor in a single, fluid motion.

'Watson, I am nothing more than a dull-witted incompetent!' he raged.

'Whatever can you mean?' I asked.

'It is not possible to explain now. Lestrade, would you, Watson and your two fine officers carry the body to the street above? There is no time to lose, for surely there are only the last glimmers of daylight left to us!'

'Glimmers, daylight? I do not understand,' the bemused inspector replied, though straining at the body just the same. We all shared Lestrade's bewilderment, yet my own experience assured me that every one of Holmes's actions and instructions would have a perfectly logical motive behind them. The climb up to street level was not made without some difficulty, so Holmes had to squeeze between us in order to support our efforts. Once there Holmes had us lay the body gently down upon the pavement and remove the covering from over Crosby's head.

Within an instant the effect of what remained of the gloaming was visible to us all. The sight of Crosby's skin awakened in my own dull reasoning something that Holmes had already foreseen. Large, unsightly red welts began to blemish the dead man's face, although, I am certain, they would have been considerably brighter and more grotesque had the sun been high.

Holmes was visibly moved at this sight. 'By underestimating the dark, devious nature of this woman, I have surely condemned this man to his untimely death,' he snarled through gritted teeth.

Although I had a greater understanding of these symptoms than Lestrade, I still felt compelled to ask: 'How has this tragedy occurred?' while the inspector merely stood there in bemused silence, his lips slightly parted.

Holmes's answer was brief and impatient.

'My own naïvety led me to enable Randell to arrange a meeting with his brother who used the forthcoming audit as the excuse, to his wife, for his having to work so late. Evidently his subterfuge failed and his wife broke in upon this meeting. An argument then ensued, as audibly witnessed by Mr Clevedon, resulting in a blow to the back of Randell's head, probably from the large spanner used to bolt down the lid of the chest on which I meditated when we were in the vault.'

'But whatever made you so certain that the body was Randell's and not that of his brother? After all, his appearance could not be more different from that of the man who visited our rooms,' I asked whilst glancing furtively towards Lestrade, who was, by now, becoming aware of our having suppressed prior knowledge.

'I am certain that, at the behest of his wife, Nathaniel swapped clothes with the corpse of his brother and then proceeded to trim his hair and beard with a pair of blunt nail scissors.' In answer to my questioning look he added: 'There were still traces of this unseemly operation on the vault floor when I examined it earlier.'

'Gentlemen!' Lestrade suddenly cried. 'There is, evidently much more about this grim affair of which you have withheld prior knowledge. This is a most serious obstruction of the police and I insist upon an immediate explanation!'

I could see that Holmes was still greatly affected by what he would undoubtedly regard as a terrible failure on his part.

'Inspector, I will be more than pleased to accompany you back to the Yard and provide you with whatever information that may be of use to you,' I offered.

Holmes placed a grateful hand upon my shoulder as he called to George, who was still waiting at the corner. 'I would suggest, Lestrade, that you cast a wider net than the Crosbys' now abandoned new home,' was his parting comment.

As an interesting postscript, I should mention that within a few days, of Randell's murder, a more potent motive than simply withholding his allowance was revealed to us by virtue of the completion of the bank's audit report. This revealed a shortfall of funds of close to £30,000! I can also reveal that the mortgage, on their new home was in default from the very first month and that their present address is still, alas, a complete mystery.

Holmes will always regret having underestimated Crosby's appalling wife and most certainly this incident has done nothing to dispel my friend's almost pathological mistrust of the female gender of our species.

THE MYSTERY OF THE
MUMBLING DUELLIST

'A third case worthy of note is that of Isadora Persano, the well-known journalist and duellist, who was found stark staring mad with a matchbox in front of him which contained a remarkable worm said to be unknown to science.'

(*The Problem of Thor Bridge* by A. Conan Doyle)

My initial introduction to the Isadora Persano affair occurred during the conclusion of the adventure of the Red Leech. Just a few moments before the murder of Crosby was brought to our attention I came upon Holmes, who was hunched in deepest concentration over a glass jar containing a most singular-looking worm.

The tragic demise of poor Crosby had left me with a feeling of forlorn emptiness for a while, which was only dispelled when I eventually returned to my old rooms at Baker Street, to find my friend Sherlock Holmes still engrossed by that unusual specimen.

On this occasion, however, the object of his attention was not to be found within a jar, for its dismembered parts were now dispersed amongst various items of laboratory apparatus with which Holmes had completely littered the room. Furthermore, a murky green liquid, which I subsequently discovered was a sample of the creature's blood, was merrily simmering over a Bunsen flame The noxious smell that this emitted was overwhelming and in an instant I threw open the curtains and raised the sash to allow some of this to disperse.

Once I had recovered my breath I turned to face my friend, I found him laughing in my direction.

'Really, Watson, it has long been a source of puzzlement to me that a man of medicine can be so encumbered with faculties as sensitive as yours. Surely a soup of worm's blood mixed with a touch of morphine is not such a heady brew?'

'You must have the constitution of a locomotive,' I retorted breathlessly. Then, once I had replenished my lungs with fresh air from the open window, I asked: 'Would you mind explaining to me the purpose behind this toxic experiment?'

'No, not at all, old fellow. This little notion of mine has done nothing to improve my understanding of the case, so therefore I can now extinguish the flame that you find so troublesome. For me to explain the reasons for all of this might, however, take some little time.' Holmes kept his promise, only to replace those fumes with some from his darkest old shag.

'My practice is somewhat slack at present, so therefore I have all the time that you might need to expand upon this problem. I assume that there *is* a case at the root of this experiment?' I asked whilst preparing a pipe of my own.

'Your assumption is correct and, if I know my friend Watson and his penchant for such things, it will prove to be a case that will ultimately find pride of place amongst the crowning jewels of your collection. What do you know of Isadora Persano?' Holmes asked of me as I took to my seat opposite his own.

'Unless I am very much mistaken, he is a highly respected journalist who has long specialized in affairs of international intrigue,' I replied.

'Anything more?' Holmes prompted.

'I believe that he freelances, because I remember reading reports from him in both the *Daily Telegraph* and *The Times* However nothing has been received from him for some time now and he is feared lost somewhere in Central America, as I recall.'

'Excellent, Watson! Evidently there is much to be gained from residing over the premises of a quiet practice, for you are certainly well read and your knowledge is accurate, albeit incomplete. I could also add to your fountain of understanding the fact that he is as well known, within the confines of certain clandestine circles, as being one of the last duellists in Europe. Furthermore and to complete your pocket biography of the man, you should also know that he has not disappeared in Central America as was at first supposed. He is to be found within these shores, but, sadly, he has also been diagnosed as insane!'

Before I was able to question him further, Holmes called down to Mrs Hudson for some tea and Chelsea buns. He ushered me into my old chair, before a cheery fire and relit his pipe from a small glowing coal. From the very moment that the last crumb had been devoured and the weary land-lady had been unceremoniously ushered from the room, Holmes's countenance assumed a more intense aspect and I was certain that his attention was now to be firmly focused upon the unfortunate journalist.

'I should begin by informing you of how I came to be in possession of a sample of a worm, deemed by the authorities to be hitherto unknown to science.

'An old acquaintance of mine, Hubbert Greene, who is currently employed as a valet at Browne's Hotel, came upon Persano, apparently in a state of torment, as he sat at his desk in one of the more discreet suites that Browne's has to offer.

'Greene had been obliged to use his pass key because Persano had not ventured from his room for two full days and Greene wished to allay his misgivings without creating a furore. Upon gaining access to Persano's suite the vision that confronted him caused Greene to collapse into a chair, where he remained dumbstruck for at least thirty-five minutes. After that he was able to gather his thoughts once more.

'Watson, you must understand that this is a man who once served with the Fusiliers, and is therefore not usually troubled by an over-sensitive disposition. But he was deeply affected by the sight of a strong, intelligent and sophisticated man of the world sitting at his desk, rocking himself back and forth whilst mumbling incoherently into his own saliva.

'In silence and with stealth, Greene stole towards the tormented guest in an attempt to make sense of the ramblings that he was murmuring, but in vain. He then followed the intense gaze of Persano's reddened eyes and soon recognized the object of his unremitting glare. Amongst the clutter of spilled food and crumpled paper, all that remained of incomplete letters and abandoned articles, nestled a half-opened wooden matchbox. Therein lay the subject of the very same experiments that you have found so abhorrent today.'

'I presume that the intention behind your experiments

was to establish why a man should be driven to insanity by so innocuous-looking a creature?' I asked.

'Of course, although I also wished to discover why the authorities categorized it as "unknown to science". I completed part of my task in the library at the Natural History Museum. Here I was able to establish that in the rituals of various indigenous peoples of Central America there is a form of punishment, performed on those persons found guilty of acts of infidelity, which involves the insertion of a large worm into the ear of the victim. When threatened, these creatures excrete a poisonous fluid that often induces a lingering, painful death. However, this outcome is by no means inevitable, but anyone who survives is rendered permanently insane! Rather suggestive, wouldn't you say?'

'Good heavens, Holmes! It is more than suggestive; surely you have the full and definitive explanation. The authorities who, I presume, retained a portion of the worm for their own investigation, obviously did not delve into the matter as vigorously as you did yourself, before dismissing the creature as unknown. Furthermore, we know that Persano's last reports came from the very region where the worm ritual is performed. What further confirmation do you require?'

'Watson, I am sorry to have bored you with so mundane a topic. There is surely no good reason for delving further into this affair.' Holmes turned his head sharply away and crossed his arms in a display of feigned indignation.

'Well, I certainly apologize for having belittled your redoubtable efforts, yet there does seem to be little point in your continuing,' I responded.

'Indeed, until you come to realize that my experiments here,' he spread his arms expansively towards his apparatus, 'have proved, beyond a doubt, that the worm in Persano's matchbox does not contain the toxin in question. That it hails from the Americas is certain, although in point of fact it is as harmless as any that you might find in your garden!'

I mumbled an embarrassed apology, relit my pipe and then asked: 'Might I, therefore, humbly enquire as to the eventual fate of the unfortunate Persano?'

'I suppose there is little point in your retaining an intelligent interest in the case unless I acquaint you with all the relevant, known facts that I possess,' Holmes responded mischievously.

'I am fortunate in that Greene was able to remove a portion of the worm for my perusal, prior to the hotel management gaining access to the room. Obviously, this has allowed me to conduct my own enquiries independently of the authorities. Their investigation, as you might imagine, was somewhat less thorough than my own. To their credit, the police did remove the worm for examination, although the outcome of this was as I have previously described. As for the unfortunate Persano, well, he was unceremoniously bundled off to the nearest sanatorium where, I am certain, he will languish for the rest of his days,' Holmes concluded sadly.

'Save for the intervention of the greatest living champion of injustice!' I announced, determined to change my friend's attitude. Holmes smiled fondly, upon hearing this and immediately strode over to the doorway, from where he called down to Mrs Hudson asking her to engage a cab.

'I do not suppose that your practice can spare you for a further few hours this afternoon while I acquaint myself with the events leading to Persano's reappearance in

London?' Holmes asked, knowing full well what my reply would be.

'I am in no doubt that it can and I would be glad and honoured to accompany you upon your quest,' I responded.

'Excellent! Then you should be delighted to know that I have arranged an interview with the last person to have seen Persano before he was incommoded. I refer to the recently widowed Doña Dolores de Cassales, who is at present residing at Le Meridien. By a happy coincidence this establishment is, as I am certain you already know, but a stone's throw away from Browne's. But we must hurry. This lady will not be kept waiting and our interview has been arranged to take place in fifteen minutes' time!'

'Oh, but Holmes,' I protested as he bundled me from the room. 'I have always understood that you do not believe in the existence of coincidence.'

Holmes paused for an instant and afforded me his steeliest of glares. 'Believe me, my friend, I do not!' He then continued to bound down the stairs.

Mercifully the afternoon traffic was light and we were able to arrive at our destination a full five minutes before our appointed time. A diminutive young bellboy led us to the lady's suite on the seventh floor and quietly announced us, before hurrying away with a few bronze coins clutched in his tiny, grateful fingers.

To our surprise the room that we had been shown into was not shrouded in the melancholy darkness that we had been expecting. Neither, indeed, was the startling vision of a woman that stood before us. Doña Dolores de Cassales was tall and elegant, indeed she stood at no less than two inches shorter than Holmes did. Her dark velvet hair cascaded in waves down to her shoulders and she wore a dress of lustrous dark-green chiffon ornamented by a profusion of ruby jewellery. I could sense that even the stoic Holmes was taken aback by this vision. The lady strode purposefully towards us and offered her hand towards Holmes.

To her amusement, Holmes gently shook her hand rather than planting a kiss upon its reverse as a lady from her culture might otherwise have expected. In any event, she soon dismissed this display of British diffidence and addressed us in a gentle Hispanic accent that modulated her perfect use of English.

'Welcome, gentlemen. You must be the illustrious Sherlock Holmes! And this ...' She turned condescendingly toward me for the first time since we had entered the room.

'This, Doña Dolores, is my good friend and colleague, Doctor Watson, a man whose discretion and honour you can rely upon as assuredly as you can upon my own!' Holmes announced this with a fervour that filled me with great pride and certainly left Doña Dolores with a manner that was decidedly less haughty. With a rustle of her gown she waved us towards a brace of elegant chairs whilst she arranged herself upon a *chaise-longue*. She then rang a small golden bell and in an instant a young maid came scuttling into the room, wearing an expression of one who was used to obeying through fear, but with no respect.

The poor girl stuttered her request for instructions and when she received them, in Spanish, they were delivered in a tone that was cold and harsh.

To our surprise the girl placed a long, dark cheroot between the lips of her mistress and then proceeded to light it from a slim candle.

'The girl will now bring us refreshments, but before then please feel free to smoke, gentlemen.' We bowed by way of acknowledgement and immediately produced cigarettes of our own. By the time we had smoked these the maid had returned, bearing a tray containing a carafe of red wine, three elegant gilded wineglasses and an abundantly laden silver fruit-bowl.

Once she had filled our glasses the girl was dismissed: 'Do not return for a full thirty minutes,' Doña Dolores instructed her. Holmes and myself were left with the impression that we had been informed of the precise time that had been allocated to us and to emphasize his recognition of this Holmes took a long, deliberate look at his pocket-watch.

'Doña Dolores, I am most anxious to obtain from you as much information as you might possess regarding your acquaintance, Isadora Persano, and his present plight.'

'You seem to regard this as such a simple thing that you ask of me. Mr Holmes,' the lady replied with a sardonic laugh.

'It is not my intention to cause you any distress, Doña Dolores, however my agent observed you visiting Persano at his hotel on more than one occasion, and you appear to be the only person of his acquaintance available to me.'

Doña Dolores caressed her wineglass as if it were a precious jewel before taking a long drink from it, all the while staring into Holmes's eyes as if by doing so she were able to discover his intentions. Evidently satisfied that Holmes had no malicious intent, she set down her glass and Holmes indicated that I should now bring out my notebook.

'I first came to Señor Persano's acquaintance when my husband took up his post at the Spanish consulate in the capital city of Guahanna, a small Central American republic. This appointment was viewed by many as a great honour. However, these are very volatile and dangerous days for Guahanna and my husband was convinced that he had been manoeuvred by his enemies, into a position from which he could not possibly emerge with any credit.'

'Which enemies would these be, Doña Dolores?' I asked quietly.

She glanced keenly towards me, as if deciding whether I was worthy of a reply. Evidently I was.

'Doctor Watson, every ambitious politician creates enemies as he builds his career, very often unwittingly, and my dear husband Francisco was no different, in that respect, from any other. Whether or not he was correct in his assumption, Francisco gradually convinced himself that this was so. Consequently, as the People's Revolution gathered pace his conviction transformed into paranoia and he saw a personal enemy behind the barrel of every musket. He began drinking wine most heavily and he barricaded himself in his room, while the flames of revolution erupted on every street corner.

'It was at this time that Isadora Persano arrived in Guahanna, and he soon presented himself at our door. As a freelance journalist it was his duty to establish what steps my husband had taken to safeguard the lives and security of expatriate Spanish citizens who still lived in Guahanna City.

'My first thought was to close the door in his face, for I was convinced that any article he might write concerning Francisco and his current condition would damage his career beyond redemption. Yet there was something in his presence and manner that evoked a feeling of trust within me. Although he was not much older than I, perhaps forty-five years of age at most, his years of travelling and the witnessing of the many harrowing events that he had reported upon had wearied his dark taut features.

'His eyes told of a great knowledge and wisdom and the soft tones of his voice had a strangely calming effect upon both me and, subsequently, upon Francisco. Oh yes, *Señores*, despite the brevity of this meeting, I took a leap of faith and allowed Persano access to my husband's room. Francisco panicked at first and refused to unlock the door. However, after a few moments of patient persuasion Persano's voice had the same effect upon Francisco as it had done upon myself, and Francisco turned the key.

'The transformation upon my husband, within but a half-hour of their first meeting, was nothing less than miraculous. I had not seen him for several days and throughout that time he had neither eaten nor slept. His hair was unkempt, his features had become haggard and gaunt and his eyes were painfully bloodshot. I broke down and wept at the sorry sight of him and would surely have fainted had it not been for Persano's intervention.

'He assumed control of the situation and immediately instructed my maid to help me to my room while he sent down for a plate of food and a barber. By the time I had returned, but an hour later, Francisco resembled his old self. Alert, assured and extremely handsome, and I saw with pleasure that the large tray, which was being removed, carried only a few remains and that the wine carafe had been replaced with one of water.'

Doña Dolores paused for a moment and smiled fondly to herself as she dwelt upon these recollections. At this juncture Holmes and I allowed ourselves another cigarette and I could sense that Holmes's patience was thinning somewhat.

'Madam, you seem to have forgotten that you have allowed us but thirty minutes to complete this interview and I have yet to hear even an indication of how Persano came to his present plight.' Holmes's blunt comment more than confirmed my misgivings as to his frame of mind. However, Doña Dolores's response was not as harsh as one might have expected.

'Señor Holmes, the matter is not a trifling one. I have related this story so that you might fully understand the nature and character of the man who is now reduced to the sorry state in which he finds himself. If our interview over-laps with my other plans by five or six minutes, then so be it. However should you wish to conclude prematurely...?' Doña Dolores gestured towards the door with an elegant wave of her left arm.

Holmes laughed quietly through a plume of smoke, whilst expanding the broadest of smiles. 'Thirty-six minutes would certainly suit me well enough. Pray continue, Doña Dolores.' With an indignant rustling of chiffon, the lady picked up her tale once more.

'Within a day or two of my husband's recovery he felt able to continue with his official business once again. Persano was able to assist him in this, in an unofficial capacity of course, by virtue of the many acquaintances that he had made in Guahanna City and the local knowledge that his profession had provided him with. His influence made it possible for Francisco to convene a meeting at which he and Persano would mediate between the leaders of the various warring factions. After a few days of earnest negotiations the People's Revolution was at an end and Francisco was proclaimed as a local hero. He even received a commenda-tion from Madrid with the promise of a more prestigious posting within a few months, provided that peace was maintained in Guahanna.

'As you may easily imagine, Francisco and Persano became the firmest of friends and Persano was a constant visitor at the consulate. My husband, of course, had good reason to feel kindly disposed toward his benefactor, but then everybody who came within his orbit was similarly affected. *Señores*, I can assure you that I was no exception!'

Doña Dolores paused once more while she lit another cheroot and the inhalation from those densely packed dark leaves seemed to ease her hesitancy.

'Now to the shocking truth behind Persano's almost obsessional desire to help my poor husband,' she resumed sharply. 'As it turned out, Persano felt no sympathy at all for my husband. He used his plight as a pretext to call upon me at every opportunity. As I have already told you, I felt drawn towards him from the moment I first opened the consulate door, an action that I curse to this very day! However, and this you must believe, *Señor*, my love for my husband was as strong and heartfelt as it always had been and my thoughts, in allowing Persano access to him, were that it was entirely for his benefit.

'Persano preyed upon this weakness of mine and he set about pursuing his aim his desire for me at our every meeting. He was unrelenting and intense and gradually I could feel my resistance weakening. I instructed the servants to put him off, should he present himself, but my husband grew agitated at Persano's absence and counter-manded these instructions. By a strange irony Francisco even accused me of being selfish in my obvious dislike of the man! I did not wish to cause him distress and so I allowed Persano access to our home once again.

'I had allowed "Diablo" the opportunity to work his evil.' She paused for a moment, drew heavily on her cheroot and turned her head away as if deeply ashamed.

'Our subsequent affair was passionate, intense. At every opportunity we sought seclusion and I scolded the servants for being too diligent and attentive. I began to drink Francisco's red wine and soon lost all sense of propriety and discretion. We even found moments during the course of official civic gatherings to steal a moment or two together, and soon Francisco began asking questions. At first they were without suspicion or accusation, merely based on confusion. However, we had not allowed for the devotion of Francisco's manservant, Diego.

'He had observed our indiscretions on more than one occasion and eventually felt duty bound to inform his master of these. At first Francisco dismissed these allegations and accused Diego of harbouring an irrational dislike of the man. On another occasion, to his great shame, he even struck Diego across the face, such was his rage. Gradually, however, the body of evidence against us increased and Francisco's moments of confusion suddenly began to make sense to him.

'He eventually confronted us in the garden house, where we had arranged our latest clandestine meeting. Although it is now too late for discretion, I will only say that he discovered us at a moment when the reason for our meeting could not have been explained away or denied. Francisco would never address a word to me again.

'To his great credit he displayed neither disappointment nor emotion. He threw me to the floor as I beseeched him for forgiveness and strode purposely towards Persano, who stood his ground. They stood toe to toe, almost as mirror image, so close were they in appearance to each other. Neither spoke a word and then, to my great horror, Francisco struck Persano across his cheeks. The malicious grin with which Persano met this attack, indicated that he understood this to be a challenge to a duel.

'Persano's reaction to Francisco's attack can best be understood when you realize that Persano was as proficient with his sabre as he was with his pen. My poor husband's act of valour was nothing less than committing suicide, yet we all knew that he could not continue to live without his honour.

'The outcome of their confrontation was mercifully as swift as it was inevitable. As the challenged, Persano was able to choose the time, place and weapon. He chose dawn the following day, on an area of flat ground close to a small, mist-shrouded arroyo, a short ride from the city and, of course, he chose the sabre. With Diego as his second my Francisco would not flinch from what he saw as his duty and bravely stood his ground. I could not bear to be present, but I could see the outcome from a distance, through a chink in a covered carriage waiting above the arroyo. Out of respect for Francisco's valour, Persano parried Francisco's initial clumsy lunge and dispatched him with a single thrust to the heart.

'I sobbed uncontrollably for what seemed to be an eternity and yet remained within my carriage to receive Persano. To my horror he and his second merely rode silently past my carriage without giving me a single glance. He would not disgrace Francisco's act of honour by acknowledging the cause of his death. Diego's reaction was even more terrible for he did ride up to my carriage and then raged and cursed me in the most awful terms imaginable!

'Diego would not return to the consulate and although I would never see him again, the hatred and vileness of his words will remain with me forever.

'After Francisco's funeral, which was attended by all the local dignitaries, I spent the next few weeks in packing up all our possessions while I awaited instructions from Madrid. During all that time I heard not a word from Persano and I shrouded myself in a cloak of guilt and remorse.

'At last I received a message from an acquaintance of mine, who worked for *The Times* in London, that Persano had refused to dispatch another word from Guahanna and had fled to London where he had become a virtual recluse. The Spanish government had arranged for our things to be shipped to my family home, close to Cordoba, while I, with a single maid and a small trunk, headed for London.

'It is still not clear to me what my true intention was, once I had decided to follow Persano to London. Part of me wanted to believe that I wished to absolve him of all guilt for the slaying of my husband, for he was as much a man of honour as my husband had been. Yet, a part of me also knew that I still longed for the warmth and passion of his embrace and the soothing tones of his voice.'

Sensing that Holmes's mood was darkening with an edgy, frustrated embarrassment, I now felt compelled to interrupt Doña Dolores's enthralling narrative. I should also point out here that Holmes had already explained to her the nature of Persano's malaise, as a means of securing this interview.

'Doña Dolores, never before have we heard a more honest, heartfelt account of personal tragedy and we are grateful for that. However, in order for us to alleviate Persano's present plight, it is important that you explain the outcome of your meetings with him here in London. We understand that you have visited him on more than one occasion. I trust that our information is correct?'

I observed Holmes smile at me out of gratitude, and we each lit another cigarette as we awaited her reply. We knew that our allotted thirty minutes had been reached because the maid suddenly reappeared. However, she was soon dispatched again, with as much 'charm' as when she had been originally summoned. The maid bustled nervously from the room and Doña Dolores turned to us once more.

'Your information is correct, *Señor* and, to my eternal shame, it is true that twice I visited his room and twice I found this once magnificent man now so consumed with guilt and remorse that he could barely bring himself even to look upon me. Guilt for having betrayed the trust of a man to whom he had pledged and given his support, remorse for having slain this same man so callously, by a means masquerading as a duel. Only his misguided code of honour could have induced him to perform such a deed and this, he swore, he would now renounce. He would, henceforth, pledge himself to a life of abstinence, devoting his gift of literacy to promote goodly deeds.

'Twice I beseeched him to reconsider his pledge, attempting to rekindle memories of the special time that we had been granted and twice he gently pushed me aside. It was not that he blamed me for that which had occurred, although all the saints know that he should have done, but because his new life held no place for a woman such as I. He spoke with such clarity and sincerity that on my second visit I promised never to return. Even now I am packed and ready to return to Cordoba, although I will not embark until I am certain that Isadora has been restored to health.'

I could sense that Holmes deplored the wretched role that Doña Dolores had played in the tragic events unfolded in her narrative. Nevertheless, when he next addressed her it was in his gentlest of tones.

'Doña Dolores, you have already mentioned Persano's guilt-ridden state of mind, yet he also appears to have spoken with remarkable clarity. Was there anything in his manner or appearance that left you feeling anxious for his mental well-being?'

'Señor Holmes, although his words were not those of my Isadora of old, they were spoken with a calm serenity. I left his rooms feeling distraught and disappointed, but I did not feel anxious for him.'

'One final question then, if you would permit, Doña Dolores?' Holmes asked as I was closing my book. 'Please think back carefully before you give your answer. Were there any unusual objects or artefacts in Persano's room, that seemed out of place or inexplicable?'

A look of annoyance flashed across the lady's face at the mere suggestion that her answer would be anything other than accurate. However she did Holmes's bidding and certainly took her time before replying. Sadly, though her answer was in the negative. She shook her head emphatically and rang her small bell once more, indicating that our time with her was at an end.

'I cannot assist you any further, gentlemen. I implore you, however to inform me of any news that you may be able to gather. *Adios!*' She turned away from us suddenly and immediately began to scold the poor maid who had just responded to the summons of the bell. We made a hurried, unceremonious exit and a few moments later were seated in a cab bound for Scotland Yard.

Despite the unsatisfactory conclusion to the interview Holmes appeared to be surprisingly animated once we got under way. He rubbed his hands together excitedly and inclined towards me whilst leaning upon his bony knees.

'So, Watson, you are certainly the undoubted expert when it comes to the behaviour of the fairer sex. Would you say that the intimidating *Señora* was telling the truth?'

'Well, judging by your description of her it would seem to indicate that you have already drawn your own conclusions!' I chuckled. 'However, I would say that I have yet to hear of a more honest and heartrending account of an illicit affair than that of the Doña Dolores Cassales. Which aspect of her story do you find so hard to believe?'

Holmes stared at me in silence for a moment, and then slowly leant back in his seat once more whilst he lit his pipe. 'All of it and none of it,' he whispered, almost to himself.

'Oh, come along Holmes, surely this time you go too far?!' I cajoled.

Without replying and when we were close to our destination, Holmes suddenly rapped on the roof of the cab with his cane and asked the driver to pull over next to the Embankment.

I asked the driver to wait when Holmes leapt from the cab and then made his way to the river. He lit his pipe and gazed over the broad expanse of the Thames.

'I had hoped that the tidal breeze might clear my head of that woman's conundrums,' Holmes replied to my questioning glances. I did not pursue his earlier inscrutable mutterings, for I knew that once his present state of mind came upon him a few moments of silence would be more conducive to extracting an answer from him.

'You thought my earlier reply to be both evasive and unnecessarily enigmatic, did you not?' Holmes asked suddenly while he was emptying his pipe against the embankment wall.

'I cannot deny it.'

'Well then, I shall attempt to unravel it.' He smiled. 'I found it impossible to doubt the validity of everything that the lady told us. It all rang true and besides, what type of mind and wild imagination could have contrived such a tale? However, her story contains nothing that can aid us in our quest for the truth. Her behaviour, upon reaching London, contradicts everything about her character that we have learnt so far. As for Persano's transformation from a world-weary adventurer and duellist to a man devoted to abstinence and philanthropy, well that certainly beggars belief!

'But then why should she lie, having just bared her very soul to us? Perhaps their experiences in Guahanna had proved to be an epiphany for them both? No!' Holmes shrieked and then slapped his forehead with the palm of his hand, in frustration. 'This affair is not yet clear to me and why is there no poison in the worm?' Holmes's voice tailed away to a whisper and he gestured for me to follow him whilst he made his way slowly back to the cab.

Upon arriving at the Yard a short while later, we were not a bit surprised to find Inspector Morrison seated at his desk. Inspector Morrison was not a detective whose path we had not crossed very often in the past. Indeed, as he now approached his late middle age, the reputation that he had acquired for preferring his desk-bound duties to those of a more active role, was gaining more credence. However, I see from my notes that on the one occasion on which we had collaborated, a tale that I have christened the *Callous Chorister*, he had proved to be a most willing and able associate, if a little stolid in his approach.

He pushed back his chair and rose to attention the instant that we had entered the room and shook us both warmly by the hand. It was only when he stood up that one could observe just how disproportionately long his legs were. For when he was seated he appeared almost tiny from behind his desk, yet now he was revealed as the giant he truly was. An absurdly thin ring of red hair circled his bald pate, although this was more than compensated for by the copious amount of hair that adorned various parts of his face. The smile with which he greeted us was warm and welcoming.

'Good afternoon, gentlemen!' his voice boomed. 'To what do I owe the honour of such a visit?'

'Ha! Honour indeed, Inspector Morrison. We come regarding the Isadora Persano affair,' Holmes cheerfully responded.

'A tragic business, that,' Morrison murmured, rubbing his chin thoughtfully. 'Although I am surprised at your involvement. I was under the impression that the fate of Mr Persano had been a matter only for the staff of Browne's and Scotland Yard.'

'My involvement comes as a result of information from another source, one that I am not at liberty to divulge at present. However, with your trust and co-operation, I feel certain that a solution might be found to relieve the plight of the tragic duellist.'

'Duellist, you say? I had no idea that such a thing existed in this day and age.' Morrison exclaimed.

'Ah, so you see there are ways in which we can help each other in solving this little mystery.' Holmes smiled.

'I was not aware of any mystery. The man obviously had a disturbing experience, while reporting on that Central American business, and undoubtedly this has unhinged his mind. I am certain that this is not a unique occurrence.'

'You do not regard it as unique that an intelligent man of letters and one who has experienced so much around the globe, should be suddenly reduced to a mumbling wreck within the confines of a sedate London hotel? Surely the presence of so remarkable a worm renders this affair unique? Was there any attempt made to examine the creature?' Holmes asked.

'Indeed there was, sir, and it was pronounced that the creature was unknown to science!' the inspector replied with an air of sadly misplaced pride in his voice.

Holmes clapped his hands together with glee upon hearing this. 'Oh Watson, what progress mankind would have made had it always relied upon such scientific endeavour! Surely we would still be existing in loincloths and mud huts!'

Wearing a look of confusion Morrison shrank back into his chair. He sat there in silence while Holmes explained to him the origins and significance of the worm. I, in turn, gave him a résumé of my notes from our interview with Doña Dolores Cassales, so that Morrison was now in full possession of the facts.

'There is evidently much more to this affair than at first meets the eye,' Morrison sheepishly admitted.

'The untrained eye,' Holmes reminded him. 'However, there is still much that continues to elude even the trained eye. For example, how came the worm to be in Persano's room in the first place?'

'If the lady is to be believed and we have no sound reason

to doubt her, it certainly was not in his room when she made her second and final visit, a full twenty-four hours before Persano was discovered,' I ventured.

'If, Watson, if.' Holmes repeated quietly, whilst evidently lost in deep thought. 'Although even should we accept her story the point you make, albeit a valid one, does nothing to solve our mystery. Do not forget that Hubbert Greene's other duties would have prevented him from stating categorically that Persano did not receive another visitor during the intervening period. Neither can he confirm nor deny that a parcel was delivered during that time. It is inconceivable that Persano would have brought the creature with him.'

'You are suggesting, therefore, that a third party delivered this most unusual of gifts, presumably in the box in which it was eventually discovered,' Morrison ventured. 'Although I cannot, for the life of me, imagine who this individual might be.'

'Watson, what opinion do you hold as to the nature of the unknown visitor?'

I slowly lit my pipe whilst deliberating upon my reply to Holmes.

'Well, whoever it was certainly had intimate knowledge of Persano's intended movements. Even the press assumed that he was lost in Guahanna, until he was discovered at Browne's. Assuming that the worm had been deposited with malicious intent, the culprit would, we must conclude, have good reason for wishing Persano dead. Your research has shown that the effect of inserting the worm only brings upon mental disturbance should the venom miss its mark. My conclusion would point to someone familiar with the rites of the indigenous peoples of Guahanna. I am certain that to anyone else the worm would appear to be nothing more than just a worm.'

By now Holmes was leaning back in his chair, a satisfied smile playing briefly around his thin lips.

'This really is most excellent!' he exclaimed. 'Now, Watson, take your exposition one step further by revealing the inevitable conclusion as to who satisfies each of your criteria!'

This time I reached my conclusion in an instant. 'Of course! It has to be Diego, Cassales's servant!'

Holmes clapped gleefully and leapt to his feet, while the bemused inspector covered his desk with matches as he fumbled for a light for his pipe. Once alight the pipe helped him compose himself sufficiently to ask: 'What steps do you suggest we take in order to apprehend this individual?'

'We must presume upon his overwhelming desire for revenge. Doña Dolores told of his resentment at her affair with Persano that resulted in his intemperate ranting at her while she sat in her carriage at the site of the duel. To see his master betrayed was hard enough for him to endure, but then to witness his ritual slaughter at the hand of his cuckolder would have aroused in Diego this most vengeful of hatreds. The means of his revenge was not hard for a man from his background to arrange. I conclude he had discovered a means of extracting sufficient amounts of the poison to render the worm apparently harmless by the time I came to experiment upon it,' Holmes concluded.

'I understand, but how do you suggest we act upon our presumption of his revenge?' I asked.

'By letting it be known that Persano is now fully recovered and that his release is imminent. Inspector, I believe that a simple statement, released to all of the important newspapers, issued by the luminaries of Scotland Yard, would be sufficient, do you not think?' Holmes suggested mischievously.

For a moment or two Morrison hesitated whilst he considered the ethical implications of this action. However, the opportunity of bringing a case to its successful conclusion at the side of Sherlock Holmes soon outweighed his initial reservations. He nodded his head emphatically.

'You think that by making this Diego believe that all of the risks that he has taken and that all of his planning have come to nothing, you will provoke him into carrying out one final, desperate course of action against Persano?' he asked.

'Inspector, I am counting upon it. Irrational as his actions so far might appear to us, to leave matters unresolved would be more than he could bear. I intend to introduce myself at the asylum where I shall await Diego's further attempt upon Persano's life. I am certain that with the backing of a member of the police force and a respected medical practitioner, with their combined expertise and influence I shall be able to bring this to pass.'

Morrison and I both agreed that this was possible, although I had my own reservations regarding Holmes's safety within such an institution.

'Holmes, give this matter due consideration before you undertake this course of action. My own limited experience of such places are both harrowing and disturbing. They are not so enlightened and progressive as modern medical institutions.' While I was speaking Morrison passed me a police report that listed Persano's place of incarceration as St Jude's Hospital, Hertfordshire, one of the oldest and certainly one of the worst of its kind. This was a consideration that I immediately indicated to Holmes, yet he remained undaunted.

I continued to bring my reservations to Holmes's attention, only from a different perspective.

'Holmes, how is it that you can be so certain of Diego's guilt? After all, to travel halfway round the world and then to infiltrate one of the bastions of British gentility to avenge the untimely demise of his former employer, does appear to be something of an excessive reaction. Especially when you bear in mind the fact than he was only in Cassales' employ for a relatively short period of time.'

'Watson,' Holmes's voice dropped to barely a whisper. 'There are many other forms of attachment between two men. The esteemed and now infamous Mr Wilde has most recently brought one of these under the public gaze.'

I fully understood Holmes's meaning, yet could still not understand why he felt the need to take such drastic and unethical action merely to ensure the mental well-being of a man who had behaved so scurrilously in the first place. I soon regretted having voiced these concerns.

'Questions! Questions!' Holmes slammed the arm of his chair, while his eyes spat fire. 'You both seem to have lost sight of the fact that our main objective is nothing less than the apprehension of an attempted murderer! Now unless you intend to search the length and breadth of our expanding metropolis for a single man who has already displayed much ingenuity, I strongly suggest that you both make the necessary arrangements.'

Holmes would evidently not be dissuaded, so Morrison and I had little choice but to do his bidding. I had maintained the acquaintance of two former colleagues of mine who had diversified into the relatively new science of psychology. The combination of Morrison's influence and Holmes's fame meant that the arrangements were soon in place.

Morrison was proving to be almost invaluable. He arranged for the press to be notified to Holmes's total satisfaction and he saw to it that the constabulary, nearest to St Jude's, would set aside a room for our use should Holmes issue an urgent summons.

We checked the papers in the morning and after a light breakfast proceeded to Hanwell via Scotland Yard. As Morrison joined us in our cab he was immediately struck, as I had been earlier, by the startling change in Holmes's appearance. Gone was his normally dapper and customary black frock-coat, the shiny black shoes and the slicked-back hair. His hair was now in a dry, tousled state of disarray, his face was made up to appear older and more worn, while his garb was now the coarse light-blue uniform of a porter.

'Good morning, Inspector!' Holmes's familiar voice cheerily greeted Morrison, perhaps to reassure him that he had climbed into the right cab.

'I must say, Mr Holmes, that I really would not have known you!'

Holmes could barely suppress a self-satisfied snigger, but then composed himself long enough to light a cigarette and to reacquaint himself with the arrangements that had been put in place.

'Dr Watson and I will be safely ensconced at the local constabulary, which we shall pass in a few moments and which is situated but a few hundred yards away from St Jude's. At the very hint of danger the head porter, who is now alert to your reasons for being there, will immediately dispatch a messenger to fetch us,' Morrison offered reassur-ingly.

'That is indeed most gratifying, Inspector.' Morrison was not quite sure how to accept this comment from Holmes and we all sank back into our seats, sitting in silence for the last few moments of our journey.

It was only as we drew closer to St Jude's that I suddenly became aware of the charming rural landscapes that were unfolding all around us. Vast swathes of lush pastures, which were intermittently bordered by some magnificent birch and elm, were spread out before us, as far as the eye could see. The occasional farmhouse appeared at the summit of gentle rolling hills and small groups of cattle gathered around tiny pools of muddied water.

Then the Gothic wrought-iron gates of St Jude's unkindly blemished this vista as it slowly came into view. Its dark austerity could not have created more of a contrast had it been the portals of Hades guarding the entrance to Nirvana. Yet this was our destination and my feelings of misgiving increased with each yard of our progress. The huge gateway appeared to be all-embracing.

Each one of its weatherworn, blood-red bricks seemed to have etched, upon its gnarled surface, a tale of fear and terror from within.

We decided that it would be for the best if we pulled up some way short of the entrance. Our mission would be better served if a supposed porter were not observed arriving to work by way of a London cab! As our driver turned us around in the direction of the constabulary, I looked back at Holmes in his blue uniform, moving slowly towards the gateway and his unknown, potentially hazardous fate.

The intervening period was spent both anxiously and

tediously. Our meagre evening meal of broth and rough bread was soon consumed and cleared away. By the time that Morrison and I were into our fourth pipes the endless speculating had come full circle. The thought of Holmes, alone and in that dreadful place, chilled me to the core. Yet exhaustion eventually took over and I collapsed on to my small bunk, which seemed to be cushioned with rocks.

My sleep was both troubled and restless and therefore it was no great surprise that a sharp rapping on my ground floor window had me awake in an instant. I looked out through bleary eyes and blackened curtains and gasped at the sight before me! At first I could not be certain that the vision was reality or the remnants of a dark and vivid dream.

A white, spectral face returned my gaze and an unfamiliar tousled fringe of hair was caked in the congealing blood that had been oozing from a large gash just above the left eye. By now I was in no doubt that both the hair and the blood belonged to my courageous friend and my urgent fingers fumbled with the window lock. I flung it open noiselessly and Sherlock Holmes fell from the sill directly on to my bunk. I raced from the room to fetch some water so as to discover the seriousness of his wound.

Holmes was motionless while I cleaned his forehead and then suddenly he sat upright and irritably swiped aside the dripping sponge.

'Watson!' he snapped. 'It is merely a scratch.'

'It is somewhat more than that and, therefore, tells of some dreadful confrontation.'

'Hardly a confrontation, although I will admit to having endured a somewhat arduous evening. Watson, could I trouble you for both a cigarette and a match?' Holmes asked humbly.

I furnished him with both. 'Should we not first rouse Morrison and return to St Jude's with all speed?' I asked, suspecting that the Diego business was still unresolved.

'That will not be necessary as the matter has already reached its conclusion. Besides I do need to take stock of the evening's outcome before we involve anybody else.'

'Concluded?' I repeated, feeling somewhat disappointed at not being involved in the culmination of the case.

Holmes was standing by the window, his dishevelled outline silhouetted by the three-quarter moon that was slowly emerging from behind a distant bank of trees. Further beyond I could just make out the imposing arched entrance of St Jude's.

'Oh, Watson, I should not have doubted you, for that is indeed a most dreadful place.' Holmes said quietly, as if he had been following the line of my gaze. He gestured for another cigarette, upon which he drew long and hard before continuing.

'I do not mind admitting that during the long walk from the gateway to the main entrance, there was more than one occasion when I considered retracing my steps and the abandonment of all of our plans. However, Nathaniel Brewer had followed your instructions to the letter and was well prepared for my arrival and intentions. To avoid any owner of unwelcome eyes becoming suspicious of my motives he immediately furnished me with a mop and bucket and I spent the remainder of the day in the cleansing of those endless corridors.'

I should mention here that Nathaniel Brewer was the crotchety old uncle of a former colleague of mine, and his strict, disciplinarian regime had largely contributed to the ghastly reputation that St Jude's had acquired.

'The geography of these corridors is, I would hope, unique. They are laid out in the form of a Panopticon that ensures that any one of the rooms can be observed from each and every angle and position on the floor. The fact that each room is barred rather than enclosed by a door or wall, renders the poor devils within them as exposed as the beasts at the new Zoological Gardens, although perhaps with less dignity! In such circumstances it would be easy to conjecture that even the sanest of men would struggle to retain their sanity within those halls.'

Holmes paused for a moment and as he turned from the window to face me, I could see that he had been greatly disturbed by the experience that he was describing.

'As I carried out my chores I soon discovered that the occupant of each room was enduring a different form of suffering. One might emit a cry or a wail, another a violent scream of anger. Many sat in abject silence, almost oblivious to their surroundings and circumstances, some rocking back and forth, muttering to themselves. What they all shared, however, was their despair and degradation.

'My adopted persona only allowed me a fleeting glance of Persano at this time and he was indeed sitting on the edge of his rudimentary bed, silently mumbling to himself.' Whilst he was speaking Holmes began to remove his uniform to reveal his customary suit beneath. His hair-brush did much to restore his more familiar appearance. He even allowed me to apply a small dressing to his wound.

A brief search of the staffroom revealed two tumblers and the remnants of a bottle of whisky. A grateful Holmes found that this discovery did much to repair his fragile nerves and he even managed the most fleeting of smiles as he lit the last of my cigarettes.

'Eventually I received an opportunity to speak with Persano when I was called upon to deliver his evening meal. Alas, the effect of Diego's worm is, as yet, unabated. Persano's eyes appeared to be vague and empty and he certainly was unaware of my presence.

'Notwithstanding the apparent futility, I persisted with my questioning of the man in the hope that I might gain a response. Once or twice I detected a glimmer of light from behind those eyes and his ramblings occasionally produced an intelligible word or two. I became excited when the words Cassales and Diego disentangled themselves until I realized that they been produced at random rather than being direct replies to my questions.

'In despair I abandoned any further attempts at reaching the depths of Persano's mind. A short while later "lights out" was announced and I knew that my vigil was about to begin. I was offered the use of a room immediately opposite to Persano's, but I decided that my hiding-place should be somewhere more secluded and discreet.

'With its door held slightly ajar, a broom cupboard that was situated further down the corridor afforded me a satisfactory view of Persano and it was from here that I decided to take up my post. The discomfort of sitting on an upturned bucket ensured that I would remain awake during the long night ahead. The stench of sodden mop heads made my task the harder to endure. I could not yet be certain that Diego would even appear! I would have to console myself with the thought that the prospect of Persano's imminent release would spur Diego to one final desperate act of retribution, so certain was I that Morrison's comments to the press would prove successful.

'My only indication of the slow passage of time was the

trajectory of the moon as it shed a strange grey light through the dark and distant skylight on its journey across the night sky. This grey illumination had an unusual, almost mystical effect upon my surroundings of steel and stone.

'The moon had almost cleared the skylight by the time I became aware of the first sound that I had heard in hours, other than that of my own deep breathing and the occasional cry from one of those poor incarcerated souls. It came from the front entrance and my heart quickened when I realized that it was the sound of a cautious and furtive footstep.

'This was followed by several others and, despite his caution, the effect of the stone floor amplified them to an unacceptable level. The steps ceased and I became certain that Diego was now removing his shoes. Fortunately for me he was also casting a shadow and I abandoned my improvised seat as the shadow neared Persano's room.

'As he gradually came into view, I slowly opened the door of my hideaway and observed my quarry. He wore a set of overalls similar to my own and brandished what appeared to be a primitive knife. Although he crouched to avoid detection I could see that he was quite short and dark of skin, while his jet-black hair had been allowed to grow down to his shoulders. He turned his head suddenly, as if he could sense my presence and I now saw that his eyes were red and frantic. I can tell you, Watson, that revenge is surely the destroyer of souls!'

Holmes paused again and it was evident that he now wished that he had been more frugal with my cigarettes. I fumbled in my pockets and eventually produced a small Indian cigar, which I offered to my grateful friend.

'It was now a matter of timing. I wished for Diego to be

preoccupied at the moment that I made my move, although I did not intend for him to progress too far with his intentions either. He had, evidently, managed to procure a set of keys from the caretaker's office and I was upon him before he had the chance to select the correct one. By the way, I subsequently discovered that the caretaker had suffered a blow to the head that had rendered him unconscious for over an hour!

'Before I was able to secure him in one of my locks, Diego was alert to my approach and he lashed out at me with the huge key ring.' Holmes smiled sardonically and pointed to his forehead. 'By the way, you have made an excellent job of the dressing, old fellow.' I waved this compliment aside, for I was now most anxious to hear of the conclusion to this adventure.

'I must admit to having been taken unawares by Diego's sudden attack and those few seconds of surprise allowed him the time to make good his escape along the never-ending corridors. I lost no time in making my pursuit, yet his short legs moved at an incredible speed and I found it difficult to make up any ground. All the while the sounds of our chase aroused the inmates from their troubled sleep and a cacophony of wailing and screaming built up to an unnerving climax. This, however, did nothing to deter the stubborn man from his progress and it was only as he approached the rear exit that I was able to close upon him.

'None the less, he was through the door before I could reach him and by the time I had breathed in the chill of the night air, Diego was already well on his way up a flight of metal steps that extended to the asylum's roof. I clattered after him, not even pausing upon the numerous landings, until I had reached the uppermost level.

'Once there I stopped abruptly. It had already occurred to me that he had chosen a strange route by which to make good his escape. After all, the roof was just as far and as high as he could go! It was only when I found myself surrounded by a veritable forest of huge, brick chimney stacks that I realized how precarious my position might be.

'I knew that Diego was in hiding behind one of those stacks, with his crude weapon held menacingly poised above his head, ready to strike should I venture behind his chimney. The flat roof was strewn with shingle so I was in little doubt that he would hear even the most cautious of approaches. I had already resigned myself to another long wait, when it occurred to me that the shingle might also work to my advantage.

'You know my method, Watson and I am certain that you have studied my monograph upon "The Tracing of Footsteps?"' Holmes eyed me quizzically before continuing, while I grunted an embarrassed apology. 'Nevertheless, I soon realized that, even without his shoes, it was most unlikely that Diego could make any movement upon that shingle without leaving a mark. In total silence I raised myself so that I could lie flat upon the roof. I strained my eyes until they ached and the moon's light glistened upon the surface of the small stones.

'Sure enough, to the right of me and toward the edge of the roof, I could just make out the shape of a small naked heel! A moment or two later I confirmed, to myself the outline of another, undoubtedly heading towards the nearest stack to my right. It was now my turn to remove my shoes and I inched my way towards my quarry.

'As I drew ever closer I was determined to remain absolutely silent and even managed to hold my breath for a full three minutes! I could detect no sound of movement from behind Diego's place of hiding and I made my move. Employing a hold from the baritsu martial art, I secured the hand in which Diego was holding his fearsome weapon. He was unable to endure the pain to his pressure point and in an instant his knife clattered to the ground.

'I collected the knife in one movement, but recoiled, momentarily, at the sight of the face that now turned towards me. Understandably it was etched with intense pain yet it was the eyes, red and unseeing in their manic rage, that chilled my blood.

'He emitted a grunt of Spanish hatred and turned toward the roof's edge before I could make a move upon him. Even now I cannot say for certain whether his next action was carried out in full consciousness or not. Yet by the time that I was able to reach him, that deranged creature had hurled himself into the dark abyss.

'As he fell, I swear that I heard the word "Francisco" echo back towards me and the sound that his body made upon contact with the stone below, was audible even from that distance.

'I sank back on to my haunches for a few minutes, reflecting upon the tragedy of which I was, in a sense, the cause. Although I knew in my heart of hearts that its real cause occurred a long time ago in Central America. Slowly I made my way back down the long flight of metal steps, pausing by Diego's shattered body only long enough to confirm the inevitable result of his fall.'

Holmes had not touched his cigar, throughout the final part of his remarkable narrative and, as he put a flame to it once more, I observed the effect that his night so fraught with danger had had upon his already gaunt features.

'My dear fellow, what an awful experience to have had to endure alone. I sincerely regret that I was not there by your side,' I observed quietly.

Holmes turned and placed his hand upon my shoulder. 'Ah, but I knew that your staunch support was just a short walk down the road and that was comfort enough. Besides I must now prevail upon you to rouse the good Inspector Morrison and return with him to St Jude's to instigate the arrangements for the body. I did not even tarry long enough to inform Nathaniel Brewer of all that had occurred, so anxious was I to quit that awful place, to which I hope never to return.'

'By all means, old fellow,' I responded enthusiastically, so eager was I to be of at least some form of assistance. Morrison was quick to respond and, mercifully, produced some welcome coffees and cigarettes, which we enjoyed before our departure. I beseeched Holmes to take some rest while we were gone.

He assured me that he would take my excellent advice. However, as I was leaving the room, I turned to see Holmes sitting by the window and staring up at the waning moon. His eyes were vague, vacant and unblinking and I could only speculate as to the ravages his fearful experience this night might eventually wreak upon his already fragile constitution.